The route to your roots

D1476444

When they look back at their formative years, many Indians nostalgically recall the vital part Amar Chitra Katha picture books have played in their lives. It was **ACK – Amar Chitra Katha** – that first gave them a glimpse of their glorious heritage.

Since they were introduced in 1967, there are now **over 400 Amar Chitra Katha** titles to choose from. **Over 90 million copies** have been sold worldwide.

Now the Amar Chitra Katha titles are even more widely available in **1000+ bookstores all across India**. Log on to www.ack-media.com to locate a bookstore near you. If you do not have access to a bookstore, you can buy all the titles through our online store **www.amarchitrakatha.com**. We provide quick delivery anywhere in the world.

To make it easy for you to locate the titles of your choice from our treasure trove of titles, the books are now arranged in five categories.

Epics and Mythology
Best known stories from the Epics and the Puranas

Indian Classics
Enchanting tales from Indian literature

Fables and Humour
Evergreen folktales, legends and tales of wisdom and humour

Bravehearts
Stirring tales of brave men and women of India

Visionaries
Inspiring tales of thinkers, social reformers and nation builders

Contemporary Classics
The Best of Modern Indian literature

Amar Chitra Katha Pvt Ltd

© Amar Chitra Katha Pvt Ltd, 2000, Reprinted October 2013, ISBN 978-81-89999-51-3
Published & Printed by Amar Chitra Katha Pvt. Ltd., Krishna House, 3rd Floor,
Raghuvanshi Mill Compound, S.B.Marg, Lower Parel (W), Mumbai- 400 013. India
For Consumer Complaints Contact Tel : +91-22 40497436
Email: customerservice@ack-media.com

The route to your roots

NANDIVISHALA

These Jataka tales are a wake-up call to all ungrateful, arrogant, hypocritical and self-serving liars. Full of humour and sound advice, they reveal the tyrannical power of money, the foolishness of superstition, and the dangers of losing self-control. So, read and be entertained, and laugh as you learn. And remember, the good always triumph.

Script
Kamla Chandrakant

Illustrations
Ashok Dongre

Editor
Anant Pai

Cover illustration by: C.M. Vitankar

NANDI VISHALA

A BRAHMAN ONCE RECEIVED THE GIFT OF A BULL-CALF WHOM HE NAMED NANDI VISHALA.

HE LOOKED AFTER IT WELL, AND IT GREW INTO A FINE, STURDY BULL.

THE KIND BRAHMAN HAS BROUGHT ME UP WITH LOVING CARE, AS IF I WERE HIS OWN SON. I MUST REPAY HIM FOR ALL HIS TROUBLE.

ONE DAY—

GO TO A RICH MERCHANT. TELL HIM THAT YOUR BULL CAN DRAW A HUNDRED LOADED CARTS. MAKE A BET ON THAT FOR A THOUSAND PIECES OF GOLD.

THE BRAHMAN COULD NOT BELIEVE HIS EARS.

AM I DREAMING OR HAVE I GONE MAD? I HEARD MY BULL TALKING!

YOU ARE NOT DREAMING, MASTER. DO AS I SAY. IT WILL BRING YOU GOOD FORTUNE.

1

ARE YOU SURE I'LL WIN SUCH A BET?

OF COURSE! OR I WOULDN'T HAVE SUGGESTED IT.

SO THE BRAHMAN WENT TO A RICH MERCHANT.

SIR, WHOSE BULL DO YOU THINK IS THE STRONGEST IN THIS TOWN?

THERE ARE MANY STRONG BULLS IN THIS TOWN BUT MINE ARE THE STRONGEST.

WELL, I HAVE A BULL WHO CAN PULL A HUNDRED LOADED CARTS. CAN YOURS DO BETTER THAN THAT?

THE MERCHANT LAUGHED—

YOU MUST BE JOKING!

I'M NOT!

IT'S IMPOSSIBLE! NO BULL CAN DRAW A HUNDRED LOADED CARTS. I'M WILLING TO MAKE A WAGER ON THAT.

THE STAKE SHALL BE A THOUSAND PIECES OF GOLD!

AGREED!

ON THE APPOINTED DAY, THE BRAHMAN WAS READY WITH A HUNDRED CARTS LOADED WITH SAND, GRAVEL AND STONES.

A THOUSAND PIECES OF GOLD WILL SOON BE MINE! ADD TO THAT THE THOUSAND I'VE SAVED OVER THE PAST FEW YEARS AND I'LL HAVE TWO THOUSAND PIECES OF GOLD!

HANGING A GARLAND ROUND NANDI VISHALA'S NECK, HE YOKED HIM TO THE FIRST CART.

WITH THAT MONEY, I'LL BUY MANY MORE BULLS AND MAKE MANY MORE WAGERS TILL I BECOME THE RICHEST MAN IN TOWN! EVERYONE WILL HAVE TO BOW TO MY WISHES!

THESE THOUGHTS MADE THE BRAHMAN VERY ARROGANT AND QUITE UNLIKE HIS USUAL SELF.

COME ON, YOU RASCAL! PULL! BE QUICK, YOU RASCAL!

THE BULL WAS SHOCKED BY HIS BELOVED MASTER'S WORDS AND BEHAVIOUR.

WELL, I'M NOT THE RASCAL HE CALLS TO! I WON'T MOVE!

THE BRAHMAN BECAME FRANTIC.

WHAT'S WRONG WITH NANDI VISHALA? WHY DOES HE IGNORE MY ORDERS?

THE MERCHANT WAS JUBILANT.

HA! HA! COME ON, SIR! YOU'VE LOST A THOUSAND GOLD PIECES!

THE BRAHMAN HAD TO GO AND BRING THE GOLD HE HAD KEPT HIDDEN AT HOME.

ALL MY LIFE'S SAVINGS GONE!

UNYOKING NANDI VISHALA, HE SADLY WALKED AWAY.

LATER, AT HOME —

ARE YOU ASLEEP, SIR?

HOW CAN I SLEEP WHEN I'VE LOST ALL MY SAVINGS? I SHOULD NEVER HAVE LISTENED TO YOU!

WHY DID YOU CALL ME A RASCAL? HAVE I EVER BROKEN A POT OR GORED ANYONE OR...?

NO, NEVER, MY CHILD!

NANDI VISHALA IMMEDIATELY FELT SORRY FOR THE BRAHMAN.

ALL IS NOT YET LOST. GO AND MAKE THE WAGER AGAIN. LET THE STAKE BE 2000 PIECES OF GOLD THIS TIME. ONLY REMEMBER, DON'T EVER CALL ME A RASCAL AGAIN!

THE BRAHMAN WENT TO THE MERCHANT AND OFFERED TO MAKE THE SAME WAGER AS BEFORE—

THE MAN SEEMS TO BE A FOOL!

YOU ARE NOT CONTENT WITH LOSING A THOUSAND PIECES OF GOLD!

I AM SO CERTAIN OF WINNING THAT I'M WILLING TO BET TWO THOUSAND THIS TIME.

TWO THOUSAND! ALL RIGHT, I ACCEPT!

WHEN THE LOADED CARTS AND THE BULL WERE READY—

NOW THEN, MY FINE FELLOW! PULL THE CARTS ALONG.

WITH A SINGLE TUG, NANDI VISHALA PULLED THE CARTS...

... TILL THE LAST ONE STOOD WHERE THE FIRST HAD BEEN!

AMAZING!

YOU DESERVE EVERY ONE OF THESE GOLD PIECES!

THE BRAHMAN TOOK THE TWO THOUSAND PIECES OF GOLD AND HE WENT HOME A HAPPIER, RICHER, WISER MAN.

THE SERVANT AND THE TREASURE

ONCE THERE WERE TWO OLD LANDOWNERS WHO WERE FRIENDS. ONE OF THEM HAD A VERY YOUNG WIFE WHO HAD RECENTLY BORNE HIM A SON.

YOU ARE VERY LUCKY. YOU HAVE A SON AND HEIR TO WHOM YOU CAN BEQUEATH YOUR FORTUNE.

YES, I'M INDEED LUCKY.

BUT I, TOO, HAVE WORRIES. IF I DIE, MY SON MAY NEVER GET THE MONEY.

WOULDN'T THE SAFEST COURSE BE TO BURY MY MONEY IN THE FOREST?

IT WOULD CERTAINLY BE A WISE THING TO DO.

SO, TAKING A HOUSEHOLD SERVANT CALLED NANDA INTO HIS CONFIDENCE, THE LANDOWNER WENT TO A NEARBY FOREST AND BURIED HIS TREASURE AT A CERTAIN SPOT.

MY GOOD NANDA, WHEN MY SON COMES OF AGE, SHOW HIM THIS TREASURE. NO ONE ELSE SHOULD BE TOLD ABOUT IT.

THE OLD MAN DIED SOON AFTER. MANY YEARS LATER, HIS SON, NOW A YOUNG MAN, MET HIS FATHER'S FRIEND.

MY FATHER WAS A RICH MAN. BUT THERE DOESN'T SEEM TO BE ENOUGH MONEY LEFT TO MANAGE THE ESTATE.

BUT HE DID LEAVE A LOT OF MONEY FOR YOU, SON. DIDN'T YOU KNOW THAT?

NO! WHERE IS IT?

SOMEWHERE IN THE FOREST. ASK YOUR SERVANT, NANDA. HE KNOWS ALL ABOUT IT.

THE YOUNG MAN WENT TO NANDA.

DO YOU KNOW WHERE MY FATHER PUT HIS TREASURE?

YES, MASTER. IT'S BURIED IN THE FOREST.

WELL THEN, LET'S GO AND GET IT. I NEED IT NOW.

I'LL TAKE YOU THERE, MASTER.

SOON THEY WERE ON THEIR WAY TO THE FOREST.

NANDA IS AN HONEST MAN. HE COULD EASILY HAVE TAKEN THE TREASURE FOR HIMSELF.

WHEN THEY REACHED THE MIDDLE OF THE FOREST —

WELL, NANDA, WHERE IS THE MONEY?

SUDDENLY NANDA WHO HAD BEEN DOCILE FOR YEARS, TURNED ARROGANT AND INSOLENT.

WHAT MAKES YOU THINK THERE IS MONEY BURIED HERE FOR YOU?

THE YOUNG MAN WAS TAKEN ABACK.

WHAT'S WRONG WITH HIM? I DON'T UNDERSTAND. WHAT SHALL I DO?

I KNOW! I'LL PRETEND I DIDN'T HEAR A WORD!

HE TURNED CALMLY TO NANDA.

ALL RIGHT. LET'S GO HOME THEN.

WHAT A RELIEF! HE'S FOLLOWING ME QUIETLY.

A FEW DAYS LATER, THEY RETURNED TO THE FOREST.

STRANGE! HE DIDN'T SEEM TO HESITATE.

BUT WHEN THEY REACHED THE SAME SPOT —

YOU IDIOT! WHAT DO YOU HOPE TO FIND HERE?

ONCE AGAIN THE YOUNG MAN IGNORED NANDA'S INSOLENCE.

NOTHING! LET'S GO HOME.

WHEN WE SET OUT, I AM CERTAIN THAT NANDA MEANS TO SHOW ME WHERE THE TREASURE IS. BUT, LATER, HE BEGINS TO ABUSE ME. WHAT COULD THE REASON FOR THIS BE?

MY FATHER'S WISE OLD FRIEND SHOULD BE ABLE TO HELP.

SO HE WENT TO THE OLD MAN AND DESCRIBED NANDA'S STRANGE BEHAVIOUR.

IT'S SIMPLE! YOU SAY HE STARTS ABUSING YOU WHEN YOU REACH A PARTICULAR SPOT IN THE FOREST? THEN THAT'S WHERE THE TREASURE IS BURIED!

HOW DO YOU KNOW?

MONEY CAN CORRUPT EVEN AN HONEST MAN. THE MOMENT NANDA STANDS ON THE SPOT WHERE THE TREASURE IS BURIED, HE BECOMES A DIFFERENT MAN.

IF THAT IS SO, WHY DIDN'T HE TAKE IT FOR HIMSELF?

BECAUSE HE DIDN'T DARE!

WHAT SHOULD I DO NOW?

GO BACK TO THE FOREST WITH HIM AND WHEN HE STARTS SHOUTING, YOU....

AND THE OLD MAN TOLD THE YOUNG ONE WHAT HE SHOULD DO.

THE NEXT DAY, THE YOUNG MAN WENT TO THE FOREST WITH NANDA AGAIN. AT THE SAME SPOT, NANDA BEGAN TO ABUSE HIM.

YOU FOOL! YOU IDIOT! YOU....

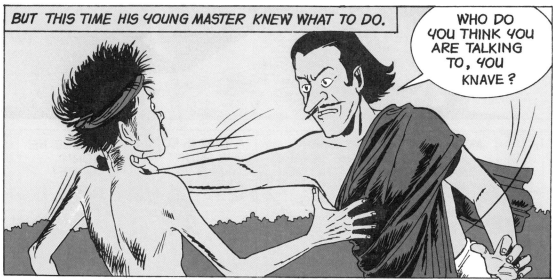

BUT THIS TIME HIS YOUNG MASTER KNEW WHAT TO DO.

WHO DO YOU THINK YOU ARE TALKING TO, YOU KNAVE?

HE BEGAN TO DIG AS NANDA WATCHED HIM DUMBLY.

DON'T MOVE FROM THERE, TILL I ORDER YOU TO DO SO.

SOON — THERE! I'VE FOUND IT!

COME HERE! CARRY THIS HOME ON YOUR HEAD.

NANDA OBEYED MEEKLY.

THE SON TOOK HIS TREASURE HOME. AND NANDA SERVED HIM FAITHFULLY TILL HIS DYING DAY.

THE WISE ONE'S ADVICE WORKED! HOW GRATEFUL I AM TO MY FATHER'S FRIEND!

THE HYPOCRITICAL SADHU

A RASCAL OF A SADHU LIVED IN A FOREST HERMITAGE ON THE OUTSKIRTS OF A VILLAGE AND HAD WON THE TRUST OF A ZAMINDAR.

NOW, THE ZAMINDAR HAD SOME GOLD WHICH HE WANTED TO HIDE FROM ROBBERS. AS HE WONDERED WHERE TO PUT IT —

I KNOW WHAT! THE SADHU IS A MODEL OF GOODNESS... AND DACOITS WOULD NEVER ATTACK A HERMITAGE!

SO HE WENT WITH HIS GOLD TO THE HERMITAGE.

HOLY SIR! WE ZAMINDARS LIVE IN CONSTANT FEAR OF ROBBERS. SO I AM GOING TO BURY MY GOLD RIGHT HERE IN YOUR HERMITAGE.

THERE'S ENOUGH GOLD THERE TO KEEP ME HAPPY FOR THE REST OF MY LIFE!

I AM LEAVING MY GOLD BURIED HERE AS I HAVE COMPLETE FAITH IN YOU. PLEASE DON'T LET ME DOWN.

IT'S NOT NECESSARY TO TELL ME THAT. WE, WHO HAVE GIVEN UP THE WORLD, NEVER COVET ANOTHER'S PROPERTY!

A FEW DAYS LATER, THE RASCAL REMOVED THE GOLD AND BURIED IT AGAIN AT ANOTHER SPOT A SHORT DISTANCE AWAY.

TOMORROW I SHALL GO AND TAKE MY LEAVE OF THE ZAMINDAR.

THE NEXT DAY —

I HAVE DECIDED TO GO AWAY FROM HERE.

WHAT'S THE MATTER? HAVE I DISPLEASED YOU IN ANY WAY?

NO, THAT'S NOT THE REASON. HE WHO HAS RENOUNCED THE WORLD SHOULD NOT LIVE IN ONE PLACE FOR TOO LONG. IT IS FORBIDDEN. SO I MUST TAKE MY LEAVE OF YOU.

WELL, IF YOU MUST GO, I CANNOT STOP YOU.

THE ZAMINDAR WALKED SOME DISTANCE WITH THE SADHU. THEN HE REVERENTLY BADE HIM GOOD BYE.

WHEN THE ZAMINDAR HAD LEFT, A THOUGHT SUDDENLY STRUCK THE SADHU —

I MUST MAKE SURE HE DOES NOT SUSPECT ME WHEN HE FINDS HIS GOLD HAS BEEN STOLEN. OUR PATHS MAY CROSS IN THE FUTURE.

PICKING UP A STRAW AND...

...STICKING IT IN HIS HAIR...

...HE RETRACED HIS STEPS.

A LITTLE LATER, AS THE ZAMINDAR SAT TALKING WITH A MERCHANT WHO HAD COME TO VISIT HIM, THE SADHU WALKED IN.

WELCOME, HOLY ONE! WHAT BRINGS YOU BACK? HAVE YOU CHANGED YOUR MIND?

NO, BUT A STRAW FROM YOUR ROOF HAD STUCK IN MY HAIR. SINCE WE SADHUS MAY NOT TAKE ANYTHING WHICH IS NOT BESTOWED ON US, I HAVE BROUGHT IT BACK TO YOU.

THE MERCHANT, HOWEVER, WAS A SHREWD MAN.

COME TO RETURN A STRAW INDEED! THIS FELLOW HAS ROBBED THE ZAMINDAR OF SOMETHING, I AM CERTAIN!

BUT THE ZAMINDAR WAS TAKEN IN.

WHAT A SENSITIVE MAN! WHY, HE WON'T TAKE SO MUCH AS A STRAW WHICH DOES NOT BELONG TO HIM!

THROW AWAY THE STRAW AND GO YOUR WAY, HOLY ONE.

AS SOON AS THE SADHU HAD LEFT —

HAVE YOU LEFT ANYTHING IN THAT SADHU'S CARE?

NOT EXACTLY. BUT I BURIED MY GOLD IN HIS HERMITAGE AND ASKED HIM TO KEEP AN EYE ON IT.

WELL, JUST GO AND SEE IF IT IS STILL THERE.

THE ZAMINDAR WENT AND SOON RETURNED.

IT'S NOT THERE! IT'S BEEN STOLEN!

THE THIEF IS NONE OTHER THAN THAT RASCAL OF A SADHU! WE CAN YET CATCH HIM IF WE'RE QUICK.

I AM AFRAID YOU'RE RIGHT!

SOON ——

THERE HE IS!

THE MERCHANT WAS THE FIRST TO REACH HIM —

CAUGHT YOU, YOU ROGUE!

WH-WHAT? I AM A HOLY MAN WHO HAS RENOUNCED THE WORLD....

IF YOU DON'T TELL US WHERE YOU'VE HIDDEN THE MONEY, YOU'LL SOON HAVE TO RENOUNCE YOUR LIFE!

MERCY, MERCY! I'LL TELL YOU WHERE IT IS!

THE SADHU SHOWED THEM WHERE HE HAD HIDDEN THE GOLD.

SO, THE STOLEN GOLD DIDN'T TROUBLE YOUR CONSCIENCE AS MUCH AS A STRAW DID!

AND GIVING THE SADHU A SOUND SCOLDING, THEY LET HIM GO.

WHAT'S IN A NAME?

IN TAKSHASHILA, THERE ONCE LIVED A VEDIC SCHOLAR WHO HAD FIVE HUNDRED YOUNG DISCIPLES.

ONE OF THEM WAS GIVEN THE NAME 'LOWLY' WHEN HE BECAME A STUDENT.

LOWLY, CAN YOU HELP ME WITH THIS SHLOKA* I CAN'T SEEM TO GET IT RIGHT.

EH? OH! IT'S EASY. I'LL HELP YOU.

LOWLY, WILL YOU HELP ME CARRY THIS?

EH! AH! TO BE SURE, I WILL.

SO HELPFUL AND KIND WAS *LOWLY* THAT ALL HIS FELLOW STUDENTS LIKED HIM.

✳ A SANSKRIT VERSE

BUT HE WAS NOT HAPPY.

WHY HAVE I BEEN GIVEN SUCH A NAME? EVERY TIME I HEAR IT, I FEEL SAD.

SO, ONE DAY, HE WENT TO HIS TEACHER.

SIR, PLEASE GIVE ME A NEW NAME WHICH SOUNDS MORE RESPECTABLE.

ALL RIGHT, MY SON. GO, TRAVEL THROUGH THE LAND WHEREVER YOUR FANCY TAKES YOU. THEN COME BACK AND I WILL CHANGE YOUR NAME FOR YOU.

SO LOWLY WANDERED FROM VILLAGE TO VILLAGE...

...TILL HE CAME TO THE OUTSKIRTS OF A CITY. THERE HE SAW A DEAD BODY BEING CARRIED BY PALLBEARERS.

WHAT WAS THAT MAN CALLED?

HIS NAME WAS 'LIFE'. SIR.

WHAT? CAN 'LIFE' BE DEAD?

WHY NOT? WHETHER HE WAS CALLED 'LIFE' OR 'DEATH', HE WOULD HAVE HAD TO DIE ALL THE SAME! A NAME ONLY SERVES TO MARK WHO'S WHO! YOU SEEM TO BE A FOOL!

PONDERING OVER THE MATTER, LOWLY ENTERED THE CITY.

SUDDENLY —

MERCY! MERCY, MY MISTRESS! I'LL TRY AND DO BETTER TOMORROW.

MOVED BY THE SIGHT, KIND LOWLY INTERVENED.

WAIT, MY GOOD WOMAN! WHY DO YOU WHIP THE POOR GIRL?

SHE IS MY SLAVE. I SENT HER OUT TO EARN MONEY AND SHE HAS COME BACK EMPTY-HANDED!

LOWLY TOOK OUT A COIN AND GAVE IT TO THE WOMAN.

HERE. KEEP THIS AND SPARE THE GIRL. SHE'LL DO BETTER TOMORROW.

AS LOWLY WALKED AWAY HE SPOKE TO A PASSERBY WHO HAD WITNESSED THE SCENE.

POOR GIRL! SHE MUST HAVE AN ACCURSED NAME!

SHE IS CALLED 'RICH'!

WHAT! AND WITH A NAME LIKE THAT SHE COULD NOT EVEN EARN A DAY'S PALTRY WAGES!

YOU SEEM TO BE A FOOL! A NAME ONLY SERVES TO MARK WHO'S WHO AND NOT WHAT THEY ARE.

PERHAPS HE'S RIGHT. YET....

MORE RECONCILED TO HIS NAME, LOWLY NOW LEFT THE CITY AND TOOK THE ROAD BACK TOWARDS TAKSHASHILA.

ON THE WAY —

I AM GOING TO TAKSHASHILA BUT I HAVE LOST MY WAY. CAN YOU HELP ME?

I AM GOING THERE MYSELF. YOU CAN COME WITH ME.

AFTER THEY HAD GONE A LITTLE WAY —

WHAT IS YOUR NAME, FRIEND?

I AM CALLED 'GUIDE'.

'GUIDE'? AND YOU'VE LOST YOUR WAY?

ARE YOU MAKING FUN OF ME? WHETHER ONE'S NAME IS 'GUIDE' OR 'MISGUIDE', ONE CAN LOSE ONE'S WAY ALL THE SAME!

EVERYONE KNOWS THAT NAMES ONLY SERVE TO MARK WHO'S WHO AND NOT WHAT THEY ARE.

YES, I HAVE AT LAST COME TO UNDERSTAND THAT TRUTH.

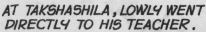

AT TAKSHASHILA, LOWLY WENT DIRECTLY TO HIS TEACHER.

WELL, DO YOU STILL WANT TO CHANGE YOUR NAME?

MASTER, I FIND THAT DEATH CAN COME TO 'LIFE', THAT 'RICH' AND 'POOR' MAY BOTH BE POOR, AND THAT 'GUIDE' AND 'MISGUIDE' CAN LOSE THEIR WAY.

I KNOW NOW THAT A NAME SERVES ONLY TO TELL WHO IS WHO AND DOES NOT GOVERN THE OWNER'S DESTINY. I AM QUITE CONTENT WITH MY OWN NAME AND DO NOT WANT TO CHANGE IT FOR ANOTHER.

THE MOST VIRTUOUS STUDENT

IN VARANASI, THERE ONCE LIVED A RENOWNED SCHOLAR WHO HAD A GROWN-UP DAUGHTER.

HE HAD A LARGE NUMBER OF YOUNG STUDENTS IN HIS CARE. ONE DAY, AN IDEA STRUCK HIM —

I WILL PUT MY STUDENTS THROUGH A TEST TO FIND OUT WHICH IS THE MOST VIRTUOUS OF THEM.

THE NEXT DAY —

I CANNOT AFFORD THE CLOTHES AND ORNAMENTS REQUIRED FOR MY DAUGHTER'S MARRIAGE. WILL YOU, MY BOYS, HELP ME OUT BY STEALING THESE THINGS FOR ME?

BUT NO ONE SHOULD SEE YOU STEALING. IT SHOULD BE DONE IN THE STRICTEST SECRECY. ONLY THEN WILL I ACCEPT WHAT YOU BRING.

FROM THAT DAY ONWARDS, THE STUDENTS STOLE VALUABLES FROM THEIR FAMILIES AND FRIENDS...

... AND BROUGHT THEM SECRETLY TO THEIR TEACHER.

I MUST KEEP WHAT EACH ONE BRINGS IN SEPARATE LOTS, SO THAT THEY CAN BE EASILY RETURNED TO THEIR OWNERS.

A FEW DAYS LATER, THE TEACHER SAW ONE OF HIS FAVOURITE STUDENTS LOOKING RATHER DEJECTED.

MY SON, YOU ARE THE ONLY ONE WHO HAS NOT BROUGHT ME ANYTHING!

YES, MASTER.

COULDN'T YOU STEAL EVEN A SMALL RING?

NO, MASTER. IT'S NOT THAT.

THEN WHAT IS IT?

YOU'LL NOT ACCEPT ANYTHING THAT IS NOT TAKEN SECRETLY. BUT I FIND THAT THERE IS NO SUCH THING AS SECRECY IN WRONG-DOING.

BECAUSE... BECAUSE, EVEN WHEN THERE IS NO OTHER PERSON IN SIGHT, I CANNOT HIDE FROM MYSELF!

THE TEACHER WAS OVERJOYED.

I HAVE FOUND THE BOY FOR MY DAUGHTER! OF ALL MY STUDENTS, HE IS THE ONLY ONE WHO IS VIRTUOUS!

MY SON, I HAVE NO NEED OF WEALTH. I HAD ONLY ASKED YOU TO STEAL AS A TEST TO FIND A VIRTUOUS MAN FOR MY DAUGHTER. YOU ALONE ARE WORTHY OF HER.

THEN HE SENT FOR ALL THE OTHER BOYS.

STEALING, EVEN FOR A GOOD CAUSE, IS WRONG. YOU HAVE FAILED THE TEST OF VIRTUE. YOU MUST NOW RETURN ALL THAT YOU HAVE STOLEN TO THE OWNERS.

THEN, ADORNING HIS DAUGHTER WITH JEWELS, HE GAVE HER IN MARRIAGE TO THE VIRTUOUS STUDENT.

THE DEADLY FEAST

A JATAKA TALE

The route to your roots

THE DEADLY FEAST

Even wily parrots risk their lives for the gentle Aushadha Kumar, a shining example of right thinking and right living described in the Buddhist Jataka tales. Scheming rivals, foolish rulers and wicked courtiers leave him undaunted. He can organise King Vaideha's security, a network of spies and a royal wedding with equal flair. So, when a deadly plot is revealed, it is Aushadha who swings into action...

| **Script** | **Illustrations** | **Editor** |
| Yagya Sharma | Ram Waeerkar | Anant Pai |

THE DEADLY FEAST

AUSHADHA KUMAR WAS A REINCARNATION OF BODHISATTVA. DAZZLED BY HIS INTELLECTUAL FEATS, VAIDEHA, KING OF VIDEHA ADOPTED HIM AND BROUGHT HIM UP.

SOON THE KING WAS SO IMPRESSED BY AUSHADHA KUMAR'S WISDOM THAT HE APPOINTED HIM HIS CHIEF MINISTER.

MAHARAJ VAIDEHA, WE MUST FORTIFY OUR CAPITAL TO PREPARE FOR ANY EMERGENCY.

DO WHAT YOU THINK APPROPRIATE, AUSHADHA.

AUSHADHA MADE ELABORATE ARRANGEMENTS TO PROTECT MITHILA, THE CAPITAL, FROM INVADERS. FIRST HE BUILT A LARGE WALL.

THE WALL HAD WATCHTOWERS FOR SENTRIES.

THEN HE BUILT THREE MOATS AROUND THE WALL. THE FIRST HE FILLED WITH WATER AND THE SECOND WITH SLUSH. THE THIRD WAS LEFT DRY.

IN THE FORTIFIED CITY HE CONSTRUCTED LARGE TANKS OF WATER AND STOCKED SUFFICIENT FOOD GRAINS.

THEN HE SELECTED A HUND-RED FAITHFUL WARRIORS AND SENT THEM TO THE HUNDRED KINGDOMS OF JAMBUDVEEPA *

WIN THE CONFIDENCE OF THE KINGS BUT DO NOT REVEAL YOUR REAL IDENTITY...

...AND SEND ME REGULAR REPORTS OF THEIR PLANS.

THE MEN CARRIED OUT AUSHADHA'S BIDDING.

* ANCIENT NAME OF INDIA

WHILE AUSHADHA WAS MAKING ARRANGEMENTS TO PROTECT THE KINGDOM OF VIDEHA, KEVATTA, THE MINISTER OF PANCHALA WAS PLANNING TO EXPAND THE DOMAIN OF HIS KING, BRAHMADATTA.

KING BRAHMADATTA IS VERY GENEROUS TO ME...

...I OWE MY PROSPERITY TO HIM...

...I MUST HELP HIM TO BECOME THE OVERLORD OF JAMBUDVEEPA. MY STATUS ALSO WILL RISE WITH HIM.

AND SO, KEVATTA WORKED OUT A PLAN.

MAHARAJ BRAHMADATTA, WE MUST INCREASE OUR FORCES.

ONE OF AUSHADHA KUMAR'S SPIES WAS PRESENT IN THE COURT OF BRAHMADATTA.

KING BRAHMADATTA IS BUSY BUILDING A LARGE ARMY. I MUST INFORM PANDIT AUSHADHA KUMAR.

KING BRAHMADATTA IS UPTO SOMETHING...

SOON, THE LETTER REACHED AUSHADHA KUMAR.

...BUT I HAVE NO MEANS OF KNOWING WHAT HIS EXACT PLANS ARE.

WELL, I HAVE THE MEANS TO KNOW.

IT IS TIME FOR MY PARROT TO ACT.

AUSHADHA KUMAR KNEW THE LANGUAGE OF BIRDS.

FLY TO PANCHALA, MY PET, AND FIND OUT THE PLANS OF BRAHMADATTA FOR ME.

AS YOU WISH, PANDIT.

SOON THE PARROT REACHED PANCHALA...

...AND ALIGHTED ON THE WINDOW-SILL OF KING BRAHMADATTA'S CHAMBER.

MAHARAJ, I WANT TO DISCUSS A SECRET PLAN.

GO AHEAD, MINISTER KEVATTA.

NOT HERE, MAHARAJ! EVEN WALLS ARE SAID TO HAVE EARS...

...LET US GO INTO THE GARDEN.

THE TWO WENT INTO THE ROYAL GARDEN. AUSHADHA'S PARROT FOLLOWED THEM.

WE HAVE BUILT A FAIRLY LARGE ARMY. YOU SHOULD NOW BECOME THE OVERLORD OF JAMBUDVEEPA.

BUT, WE ARE NOT POWERFUL ENOUGH TO ACCOMPLISH THAT.

WE CAN, MAHARAJ! BY DECEIT!

DECEIT?!

YES! WE SHALL SURROUND ONE SMALL KINGDOM AT A TIME AND THEN INFORM THE KING...

...THAT WE WILL SPARE HIS LIFE AND LET HIM RULE HIS KINGDOM IF HE ACCEPTS YOUR OVERLORDSHIP.

THE KING WILL HAVE NO OPTION BUT TO SURRENDER.

...THUS, ONE BY ONE WE SHALL ANNEX ALL THE HUNDRED KINGDOMS WITHOUT SHEDDING A DROP OF OUR BLOOD.

BUT I WILL BE OVERLORD ONLY IN NAME. AS THE KINGS WILL RULE THEIR OWN KINGDOMS.

THEY WILL NOT, MAHARAJ! AFTER THE CAMPAIGN IS OVER WE SHALL INVITE THEM TO A FEAST...

... WHERE ALL OF THEM WILL BE POISONED.

RASCAL!

AFTER THE FEAST, NO KING WILL LIVE TO CHALLENGE YOUR THRONE.

EXCELLENT!

I MUST INFORM AUSHADHA PANDIT IMMEDIATELY.

WHILE TAKING OFF, THE PARROT MADE A LOUD SOUND.

KIRI! KIRI! KIRI!

OH! WHAT A RACKET THIS PARROT MAKES!

THE ANGRY PARROT DROPPED HIS EXCRETA ON KEVATTA.

DRAT THAT PARROT.

THE PARROT FLEW STRAIGHT TO AUSHADHA KUMAR. AUSHADHA WAS PERTURBED BY THE INFORMATION.

I CANNOT ALLOW SO MANY KINGS TO DIE...

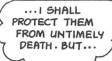

...I SHALL PROTECT THEM FROM UNTIMELY DEATH. BUT...

...BEFORE THAT I MUST ARRANGE TO PROTECT MY OWN PEOPLE.

AUSHADHA KUMAR MOVED THE CITIZENS FROM THE OUTSKIRTS INTO THE FORTIFIED CITY.

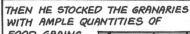

THEN HE STOCKED THE GRANARIES WITH AMPLE QUANTITIES OF FOOD GRAINS.

MEANWHILE, KING BRAHMADATTA MARCHED WITH HIS ARMY TO CARRY OUT THE NEFARIOUS PLAN CONCEIVED BY KEVATTA.

BRAHMADATTA SURROUNDED THE FORT OF A NEIGHBOURING KING, AS PLANNED BY KEVATTA.

NOW WE SHOULD SEND OUR MESSAGE OF PEACE!

SOON, THE MESSENGER REACHED THE ENEMY KING.

ACCEPT OUR FRIENDSHIP AND PROSPER OR INVITE OUR WRATH AND PERISH.

AS ENVISAGED BY KEVATTA, THE ENEMY KING SURRENDERED WITHOUT GIVING FIGHT.

IN SEVEN YEARS, SEVEN MONTHS AND SEVEN DAYS, BRAHMADATTA BECAME THE OVERLORD OF ONE HUNDRED KINGS THROUGH HIS CLEVER SCHEME.

I, KING OF ANGA SURRENDER TO YOU.

I, KING OF VANGA SURRENDER TO YOU.

I, KING OF KALINGA SURRENDER TO YOU.

I, KING OF SHRAVASTI SURRENDER TO YOU.

I, KING OF KASHI SURRENDER TO YOU.

I, KING OF MAGADHA SURRENDER TO YOU.

AUSHADHA KUMAR RECEIVED TIMELY REPORTS OF SURRENDERS OF EACH OF THE HUNDRED KINGS.

KEVATTA IS CRAFTY. BUT I AM READY FOR HIM.

KEVATTA WAS AWARE OF AUSHADHA'S CAPABILITY. SO WHEN ONE DAY KING BRAHMADATTA SUGGESTED—

WE SHOULD NOW TURN TO VAIDEHA. HIS IS THE ONLY KINGDOM NOT UNDER US.

MAHARAJ. VIDEHA IS A VERY SMALL KINGDOM.

...IT WILL BE DEMEANING FOR AN OVERLORD OF A HUNDRED KINGS TO ATTACK A TINY STATE.

ALL RIGHT, BUT WHAT ABOUT THE REMAINING PART OF OUR SCHEME...

...WHEN DO WE GET RID OF THE KINGS?

I SHALL SEND INVITATIONS OF DEATH TO THE KINGS RIGHT NOW.

THE HUNDRED KINGS RECEIVED IDENTICAL MESSAGES.

EMPEROR BRAHMA-DATTA, THE OVERLORD OF JAMBUDVEEPA, INVITES YOU TO A FEAST TO CELEBRATE HIS DIGVIJAYA.*

WHEN AUSHADHA KUMAR LEARNT THAT THE DEADLY FEAST HAD BEEN FIXED, HE DECIDED TO ACT.

TAKE A HUNDRED TRUSTED WARRIORS DISGUISED AS PANCHALAS...

... ENTER THE VENUE OF THE FEAST A LITTLE BEFORE ITS SCHEDULED TIME...

...AND DESTROY ALL THE FOOD AND DRINKS. BUT BEFORE YOU LEAVE ANNOUNCE YOURSELF AS MEN OF THE KING OF VIDEHA.

THE MEN DID AUSHADHA'S BIDDING.

WHERE IS THE SEAT FOR KING VAIDEHA?

HE IS NOT INVITED.

THAT IS AN INSULT TO OUR KING.

SINCE OUR KING IS NOT INVITED, WE WILL NOT ALLOW ANYONE ELSE TO ENJOY THE FEAST.

* CONQUEST OVER ALL

SO, AUSHADHA KUMAR'S MEN DESTROYED THE POISONED FOOD...

...AND ESCAPED ON SWIFT HORSES.

BRAHMADATTA WAS FURIOUS.

RASCALS! THEY HAVE RUINED MY PLANS.

I SHALL ATTACK MITHILA AND BEHEAD VAIDEHA.

MAHARAJ, IT WILL NOT BE AN EASY TASK...

...MITHILA IS PROTECTED BY AUSHADHA KUMAR.

WHAT CAN HE DO AGAINST THE OVERLORD OF JAMBUDVEEPA?

SO BRAHMADATTA INCITED THE HUNDRED KINGS —

THE KING OF MITHILA HAS INSULTED ALL OF US BY RUINING OUR FEAST.

WE SHALL PUNISH HIM.

YES! WE SHALL KILL HIM AND THEN HAVE OUR FEAST.

ACCOMPANIED BY THE HUNDRED KINGS AND A HUGE ARMY, BRAHMADATTA MARCHED TO MITHILA. KEVATTA WENT WITH BRAHMADATTA SO AS NOT TO DISPLEASE HIS KING.

SOON, BRAHMADATTA LAID A SIEGE TO MITHILA.

OH GOD, BRAHMADATTA WILL STORM MY FORT AND KILL ME.

BUT, AUSHADHA KUMAR, UNAFRAID LIKE A LION, INSPECTED THE SECURITY ARRANGEMENTS. HE THEN REPORTED TO THE KING.

GLORY BE TO KING VAIDEHA!

THE DAYS OF MY GLORY ARE OVER, AUSHADHA. I CAN SEE MY END CLEARLY.

DO NOT FEEL ANXIOUS, MAHARAJ. I HAVE A SOLUTION.

I SHALL SCATTER THE ENEMY JUST AS CROWS ARE DISPERSED WITH A STICK...

... OR JUST AS THE MONKEYS ARE PUT ON THE RUN BY A HANDFUL OF STONES...

... BE RELAXED MAHARAJ, FOR THE ENEMY WILL RUN AWAY LEAVING EVEN THEIR WEAPONS. BEHIND.

WHILE AUSHADHA KUMAR WAS TRYING TO ALLAY VAIDEHA'S FEARS, BRAHMADATTA LAUNCHED AN ATTACK ON THE FORT.

THE APPROACH TO THE FORT WAS MADE DIFFICULT BY THE THREE MOATS AROUND IT.

WHEN THE ENEMY SOLDIERS CAME NEAR THE FORT, VAIDEHA AND SOLDIERS SHOWERED THEM WITH STONES AND OTHER MISSILES...

...AND BRAHMADATTA'S ATTACK FAILED MISERABLY.

WHAT SHALL WE DO? SHALL WE LIFT THE SIEGE AND GO BACK?

NO, THAT WILL MEAN A LOSS OF FACE. YOU CANNOT AFFORD THAT AS THE OVER-LORD OF JAMBU-DVEEPA.

BUT HOW CAN I SAVE MY FACE?

I SHALL USE A TRICK TO GAIN A TOKEN VICTORY.

HOW?

BY RESORTING TO DHARMAYUDDHA.*

DHARMAYUDDHA!?

YES, I AS YOUR CHIEF MINISTER SHALL CHALLENGE...

...VAIDEHA'S CHIEF MINISTER AUSHADHA KUMAR TO MATCH HIS WITS WITH MINE...

...WHOEVER WINS, HIS SIDE WILL BE CONSIDERED VICTORIOUS.

HOW WILL WE KNOW WHO HAS WON?

THE VANQUISHED WILL BOW TO THE VICTOR.

BUT YOU YOURSELF ADMIT THAT AUSHADHA IS WISER THAN YOU.

YES, BUT NOT CRAFTIER THAN ME...

* BATTLE ACCORDING TO DHARMA.

16

SINCE, HE IS YOUNGER, HE WILL BOW TO GREET ME.

THE MOMENT HE DOES THAT I SHALL ANNOUNCE THAT HE HAS ADMITTED DEFEAT.

AUSHADHA KUMAR WAS PROMPTLY WARNED OF THE CONSPIRACY BY HIS SPIES.

AH! SO THAT IS YOUR GAME, KEVATTA. WE WILL SEE WHO WINS THIS BATTLE OF WITS.

ON THE DAY OF THE DHARMAYUDDHA, AUSHADHA CARRIED A PRICELESS JEWEL AS A PRESENT TO KEVATTA.

I AM SORRY PANDIT KEVATTA, THAT I COULD NOT GREET YOU EARLIER...

...BUT NOW KINDLY ACCEPT THIS GEM AS A TOKEN OF MY RESPECT.

WHILE GIVING THE GEM, AUSHADHA KUMAR DELIBERATELY LET IT FALL ON THE GROUND.

UNTHINKINGLY KEVATTA BENT DOWN TO PICK UP THE GEM.

AS SOON AS KEVATTA BENT DOWN, AUSHADHA-KUMAR PLACED HIS HANDS ON KEVATTA'S SHOULDERS AND PRESSED HIS HEAD DOWN ON THE EARTH. THE HEAD STRUCK WITH FORCE AND A DEEP GASH APPEARED ON KEVATTA'S FOREHEAD

AH!

NO! PANDIT KEVATTA, DO NOT TOUCH MY FEET...

...I KNOW, YOU HAVE ADMITTED DEFEAT. BUT I AM MUCH YOUNGER THAN YOU. SO PLEASE DO NOT BOW TO ME. RISE O ACHARYA, RISE!

THEN AUSHADHA WHISPERED TO KEVATTA —

STUPID FOOL! YOU EXPECTED ME TO BOW TO YOU.

AND THEN HE PUSHED KEVATTA AWAY WITH SUCH FORCE THAT KEVATTA FELL DOWN AT A DISTANCE.

AND IMMEDIATELY AT A PRE-ARRANGED SIGNAL AUSHADHA KUMAR'S ARMED SOLDIERS RUSHED OUT OF VAIDEHA'S FORT. KEVATTA RAN AT THE SIGHT OF THE SOLDIERS.

AND SO DID BRAHMADATTA, THE HUNDRED PANIC STRICKEN KINGS AND THEIR SOLDIERS.

KEVATTA HAS BEEN DEFEATED! RUN! RUN!

AS AUSHADHA KUMAR HAD FORETOLD, THE TERRIFIED ENEMY RAN AWAY LEAVING EVEN THEIR WEAPONS BEHIND.

THE WOUND ON KEVATTA'S FORE-HEAD LEFT A MARK. THE MARK CONSTANTLY REMINDED KEVATTA OF HIS HUMILIATION.

OH, AUSHADHA KUMAR, I WILL NOT FORGIVE YOU FOR THIS.

FINALLY, KEVATTA HATCHED A SCHEME.

MAHARAJ, I HAVE A PLAN TO AVENGE OUR INSULT.

YOUR PLAN DID NOT WORK OUT LAST TIME, KEVATTA.

THIS TIME IT WILL. FOR YOU SHALL OFFER YOUR DAUGHTER TO VAIDEHA.

ARE YOU OUT OF YOUR MIND?

NO, MAHARAJ. THIS SCHEME WILL WORK. BECAUSE...

...YOUR DAUGHTER PANCHALA CHANDI IS THE MOST CHARMING MAIDEN IN JAMBUDVEEPA.

VAIDEHA WILL BE LURED BY HER BEAUTY...

...AT THE TIME OF THE WEDDING WE SHALL KILL BOTH VAIDEHA AND AUSHADHA KUMAR.

ARE YOU SURE THE SCHEME WILL WORK?

I WILL MAKE SURE THAT IT DOES, MAHARAJ.

KEVATTA PREPARED A METICULOUS PLAN. THE BARDS SENT BY HIM SANG VERSES PRAISING THE ENCHANTING BEAUTY OF THE PANCHALA PRINCESS.

SOON, A BARD HAD AUDIENCE WITH KING VAIDEHA. A PAINTER FROM PANCHALA PRESENTED A PAINTING OF THE PRINCESS TO THE KING.

AH! WHAT EXQUISITE BEAUTY. WHAT IS THE USE OF MY BEING A KING IF I CAN'T MAKE HER MY WIFE.

LATER AUSHADHA EXPRESSED HIS DOUBTS.

MAHARAJ, YOU SHOULD NOT ACCEPT THE ALLIANCE.

WHY?

BECAUSE I THINK BRAHMADATTA IS LURING YOU THE WAY A HUNTER USES A TAME DOE TO TRAP A STAG.

THE OTHER FOUR COURT PANDITS, WHO WERE JEALOUS OF AUSHADHA KUMAR*DECIDED TO USE THIS OPPORTUNITY TO HUMILIATE HIM.

YOU ARE COMPARING OUR KING WITH A DUMB ANIMAL.

ON THE CONTRARY, YOU ARE DUMB.

YOU SIMPLY DO NOT UNDERSTAND POLITICS.

THIS MARRIAGE MUST BE SOLEMNISED. IT WILL HAVE FAR-REACHING POLITICAL ADVAN— TAGES FOR US...

OUR KING WILL BECOME THE SON-IN-LAW OF THE OVER- LORD OF JAMBUDVEEPA.

AUSHADHA WAS AFRAID THAT THE MARRIAGE WOULD LEAD TO DISASTER BUT HE DID NOT KNOW HOW TO DISSUADE THE KING.

* SEE AMAR CHITRA KATHA NOS·625

SO WHEN KEVATTA BROUGHT THE MARRIAGE PROPOSAL—

THIS ALLIANCE WILL UNITE THE PEOPLE OF PANCHALA AND VIDEHA.

I'M HAPPY TO ACCEPT THE PROPOSAL.

BRAHMADATTA AND KEVATTA ARE UP TO SOME TRICK.

SO HE SOUGHT INFORMATION FROM HIS SPY IN PANCHALA. PROMPTLY HE RECEIVED A MESSAGE—

CLEAR INFORMATION IS NOT AVAILABLE. KEVATTA AND BRAHMADATTA REGULARLY CONFER IN A CLOSED ROOM. NO OTHER SOUL WAS PRESENT EXCEPT A CAGED MYNAH BIRD.

I MUST SEND MY PARROT AGAIN.

AGAIN THE PARROT FLEW...

...AND REACHED BRAHMADATTA'S PALACE...

GREETINGS, O BEAUTIFUL MYNAH.

GREETINGS, O PARROT! WHERE DO YOU COME FROM? AND WHAT BRINGS YOU HERE?

TO EXTRACT THE VITAL INFORMATION, THE PARROT LIED TO THE MAINAH —

I AM THE ROYAL PARROT OF SHIVI*. I'M LOOKING FOR A SUITABLE BRIDE FOR MYSELF.

WELL, HAVE YOU FOUND ONE?

YES, IF YOU AGREE THEN I HAVE...

WHY SHOULD I AGREE?

BECAUSE MARRIAGE LEADS TO ETERNAL HAPPINESS.

NOT ALWAYS.

WHAT DO YOU MEAN?

THE MARRIAGE OF THE PANCHALA PRINCESS TO KING VAIDEHA, IS GOING TO CAUSE UTTER MISERY.

HOW?

VAIDEHA WILL BE KILLED, WHEN HE COMES FOR THE WEDDING.

* AN ANCIENT KING

WHEN AUSHADHA KUMAR LEARNT OF THE DASTARDLY PLAN HE TRIEL TO DISSUADE VAIDEHA AGAIN. BUT VAIDEHA WAS NOT PREPARED TO LISTEN.

YOUR PARROT IS A STUPID BIRD.

BUT, PARDON ME, MAHARAJ.

NO, I'LL NOT DISCUSS THE MATTER ANY FURTHER.

AS YOU WISH, MAHARAJ.

THE KING IS BLINDED BY HIS DESIRES. BUT AS HIS MINISTER IT IS MY DUTY TO PROTECT HIM.

SO, AUSHADHA KUMAR WENT WITH THE ADVANCE PARTY TO THE PANCHALA CAPITAL.

MAHARAJ BRAHMADATTA, I HAVE COME TO MAKE ARRANGEMENTS FOR A GRAND WEDDING.

LET US KNOW IF YOU NEED ANY HELP.

I DO, I NEED A HOUSE AND SOME LAND TO BUILD A LODGE FOR THE WEDDING PARTY.

THAT WILL BE ARRANGED.

SO AUSHADHA WAS GIVEN A HOUSE NEAR THE PALACE TO STAY AND A PIECE OF LAND OUTSIDE THE CITY.

WHY DID YOU ALLOW HIM TO STAY NEAR THE PALACE?

SO THAT WE CAN KEEP A WATCH ON HIM.

AND WHY DID YOU GIVE HIM LAND OUTSIDE THE CITY?

BECAUSE IT WILL BE EASY TO SURROUND AND FINISH THEM OFF THERE.

ONCE AUSHADHA WAS SETTLED, HE STARTED TWO WORKS SIMULTANEOUSLY—THE CONSTRUCTION OF A PALATIAL HOUSE OUTSIDE THE CITY...

...AND THE DIGGING OF A TUNNEL FROM THE HOUSE WHERE HE WAS STAYING.

THE TUNNEL WILL HAVE TWO OUTLETS—ONE IN THE HOUSE THAT WE ARE BUILDING...

...AND THE OTHER NEAR THE RIVER.

SOON, ONE END OF THE TUNNEL OPENED IN THE NEW HOUSE...

...AND THE OTHER IN THICK BUSHES NEAR THE RIVER.

WHEN ALL ARRANGEMENTS WERE MADE, KING VAIDEHA WAS SUMMONED TO PANCHALA.

SOON AFTER VAIDEHA ARRIVED, HIS HOUSE WAS SURROUNDED BY BRAHMADATTA AND HIS MEN.

UNAWARE OF THE TREACHERY, AND TIRED FROM THE JOURNEY, VAIDEHA WAS SLEEPING.

BUT AUSHADHA KUMAR WAS ALERT. HE PUT THE NEXT PART OF HIS SCHEME INTO OPERATION.

DISGUISE A FEW MEN AS PANCHALA SOLDIERS AND GO TO BRAHMA-DATTA'S PALACE THROUGH THE TUNNEL.

AS INSTRUCTED THE MEN WENT TO BRAHMADATTA'S PALACE AND ADDRESSED HIS QUEEN.

O QUEEN! VAIDEHA HAS BEEN KILLED...

...KING BRAHMADATTA HAS ASKED ALL OF YOU TO JOIN HIM IN THE FEAST CELEBRATING THIS VICTORY.

THUS THE PANCHALA QUEEN AND THE PRINCESS WERE TRICKED INTO ACCOMPANYING AUSHADHA KUMAR'S SOLDIERS.

MEANWHILE, VAIDEHA WAS AWAKENED BY THE NOISE MADE BY THE PANCHALA ARMY.

BLOCK ALL ROUTES OF ESCAPE.

WHAT IS THAT?

OH GOD, WE SHALL ALL BE BUTCHERED NOW.

WHEN DESIRES CLOUD THE SENSES THEY LEAD TO MISERY, MAHARAJ!

WHAT SHALL WE DO NOW?

SENAKA AND OTHER PANDITS UNDERSTAND POLITICS BETTER THAN I DO, MAHARAJ. LET THEM GUIDE YOU.

WHEN CONSULTED, ALL THE TERRIFIED PANDITS COULD DO WAS LAMENT.

BRAHMADATTA WILL TORTURE US TO DEATH.

LET US KILL OURSELVES BEFORE THAT.

YES, DEATH WILL BE LESS PAINFUL THIS WAY.

OH, GOD! IS THERE NO WAY TO ESCAPE?

THE KING IS TERRIFIED... I SHOULD REASSURE HIM.

THE WAY TO SAFETY LIES UNDER THE GROUND, MAHARAJ.

UNDERGROUND!

YES! PLEASE STEP THIS WAY.

THROUGH THE TUNNEL AUSHADHA KUMAR TOOK THE KING AND THE PANDITS TO WHERE THE PANCHALA QUEEN AND PRINCESS WERE HELD BY HIS MEN.

MAHARAJ, YOUR BRIDE AND HER MOTHER ARE WAITING FOR YOU HERE...

...PLEASE TAKE THEM WITH YOU TO MITHILA. THE BOATS ARE WAITING.

A MUCH RELIEVED VAIDEHA RUSHED TOWARDS THE BOAT.

COME ON AUSHADHA, LET US NOT WASTE TIME.

I AM NOT COMING, MAHARAJ...

...MY MEN ARE TRAPPED BY THE ENEMY. I CANNOT LEAVE THEM BEHIND.

NEXT MORNING WHEN BRAHMADATTA BARGED INTO THE HOUSE WHERE VAIDEHA WAS STAYING—

WHERE IS VAIDEHA?

HE HAS GONE TO MITHILA WITH YOUR WIFE AND DAUGHTER.

WHEN BRAHMADATTA LEARNT THE TRUTH HE BECAME LIVID WITH RAGE.

CUT OFF HIS NOSE, CUT OFF HIS HANDS, CUT OFF HIS HEAD.

THINK CAREFULLY BEFORE YOU DO ANYTHING RASH, O KING...

...BECAUSE, IF YOU CUT OFF MY NOSE, MY KING WILL CUT OFF THE NOSE OF YOUR QUEEN.

WHATEVER YOU DO TO ME THE SAME WILL BE DONE TO YOUR WIFE.

YOU ARE BLUFFING!

THEN CALL MY BLUFF.

BUT BRAHMADATTA DID NOT DARE TO PUNISH AUSHADHA AT THE RISK OF HIS WIFE'S LIFE.

SOON, AUSHADHA RETURNED SAFELY TO MITHILA WITH ALL HIS MEN.

HOW DID YOU MANAGE TO ESCAPE CERTAIN DEATH?

MAHARAJ, THE BRAIN IS MIGHTIER THAN BRAWN. WISDOM ALWAYS TRIUMPHS.

THE END.

TINKLE **KARADI TALES** From the house of Amar Chitra Katha and Tinkle **BRAINWAVE** SCIENCE IS JUST A GAME  **Bright Start**

9 amazing offers on your favourite reads!

Get
additional 20%
off on
ACK Complete
Collection.
Code: ACKCC20

www.amarchitrakatha.com

Get
additional 15% off
on any ACK Complete
Collection
Volumes (1, 2 & 3).
Code: ACKV15

www.amarchitrakatha.com

Get
flat 15% off on all
India Book House
books on
amarchitrakatha.com.
Code: IBHACK15

www.amarchitrakatha.com

Get
additional 20% off
on 1 year Subscription
of Tinkle magazine
Code: TINKLE20

www.amarchitrakatha.com

Get
additional 25% off
on 1 year Subscription
of Tinkle Combo
Code: ACKTC25

www.amarchitrakatha.com

Get
additional 10% off
on 1 year Subscription
of Brainwave
Code: BRAINWAVE10

www.amarchitrakatha.com

Get
flat 30% discount
on all Karadi
Products on
Amarchitrakatha.com.
Code: KARADI30

www.amarchitrakatha.com

Get
additional 15% off
on 1 year Subscription
of Nationa Geographic
Code: NATGEO15

getnationalgeographic.com

Get
additional 5% off
on 1 year Subscription
of National Geographic
Magazine and National
Geographic Traveller India
Combo
Code: NGC05

getnationalgeographic.com

How to Redeem:
1. Log on to www.amarchitrakatha.com for Amar Chitra Katha offers and www.getnationalgeographic.com for National Geographic offers
2. Select the products you wish to buy and add to your shopping cart.
3. Proceed to "Checkout & Pay" and enter the coupon code in discount Code section. Click on the "Verify" button & proceed with the address and payments details.

Terms and Conditions:
1. Customers can redeem the coupon code only at our online stores .
2. To avail the discount, customer will have to submit the coupon code at the checkout page.
3. ACK Media reserves the right to change or withdraw the offer and/or the promo codes, anytime, at the sole discretion of the management.
4. All standard Terms & Conditions available at amarchitrakatha.com & getnationalgeographic.com will apply.

AMAR CHITRA KATHA

Special volumes that bring the most popular classics of all time in a collector's edition.

AMAR
CHITRA
KATHA

BATTLE OF WITS

TALES OF THE BODHISATTVA AUSHADHA KUMAR

The route to your roots

BATTLE OF WITS

He was just seven years old, but Aushadha Kumar already had the wisdom of the Buddha. Unscrupulous courtiers were terrified that he would oust them from positions of power and comfort, and tried every trick to keep him away from their king. But Aushadha was needed at court for the greater happiness of the kingdom. Eventually, nothing and no one could subdue his destiny.

Script	Illustrations	Editor
Yagya Sharma	Ram Waeerkar	Anant Pai

Battle of Wits

LONG LONG AGO MITHILA WAS RULED BY A KING NAMED VAIDEHA. ONE NIGHT HE HAD A STRANGE DREAM. FOUR PILLARS AS HIGH AS THE WALLS OF HIS FORT WERE BURNING BRIGHTLY IN THE COURTYARD OF HIS PALACE.

SUDDENLY A TINY FLAME APPEARED AMIDST THE BURNING PILLARS AND...

...GREW TALLER AND TALLER TILL IT DWARFED THEM, THE FORT, THE PALACE AND ALL.

1

THE KING WOKE UP TREMBLING.

OH GOD! WHAT A DREAM!

THE NEXT MORNING HE CONSULTED SENAK, PUKKUS, KAVIND AND DEVIND, THE FOUR PANDITS OF HIS COURT.

SENAK, WHAT DOES MY DREAM SIGNIFY?

ONLY GOOD, MAHARAJ.

THE FOUR BURNING PILLARS YOU SAW IN YOUR DREAM REPRESENT PUKKUS, KAVIND, DEVIND AND ME. AND...

... THE BRIGHT FLAME FORETELLS THE ADVENT OF A GREAT SOUL WHOSE WISDOM WILL SURPASS OUR COMBINED KNOWLEDGE.

WHEN WILL THIS GREAT SOUL BE BORN?

YOUR DREAM INDICATES THAT HE ENTERED THE WOMB OF A NOBLE MOTHER LAST NIGHT.

2

SENAK WAS RIGHT. THE BODHISATTVA* HAD ENTERED THE WOMB OF SUMANA DEVI, WIFE OF SHRIVARDHANA, A WEALTHY RESIDENT OF YAVAMAJJHAKA VILLAGE.

TEN MONTHS LATER, SUMANA DEVI GAVE BIRTH TO A RADIANT SON.

OUR SON'S FACE GLOWS WITH DIVINITY.

WHAT IS HE HOLDING IN HIS HAND?

I'LL OPEN IT AND SEE.

WHEN THE FIST WAS OPENED—

IT'S JUST A PIECE OF WOOD.

*SEE INTRODUCTION

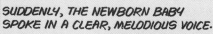

SUDDENLY, THE NEWBORN BABY SPOKE IN A CLEAR, MELODIOUS VOICE.

THIS PIECE OF WOOD POSSESSES MYSTERIOUS POWERS OF HEALING.

FOR THE PAST SEVEN YEARS, SETH SHRIVARDHANA HAD BEEN SUFFERING FROM FREQUENT BOUTS OF HEADACHE.

THE NEXT TIME I HAVE A HEADACHE I'LL TRY THIS OUT.

THE VERY NEXT DAY HE HAD ONE. HE QUICKLY BROUGHT OUT THE PIECE OF WOOD, RUBBED IT ON A GRINDING-STONE...

... AND APPLIED THE PASTE TO HIS FOREHEAD. AND LO!

IT'S GONE! MY HEADACHE HAS GONE!

I'LL MIX THIS IN WATER AND DISTRIBUTE THE MIXTURE TO THE AILING.

4

FAME OF THE HERB SPREAD, AND AILING PEOPLE FROM NEAR AND FAR FLOCKED TO SHRIVARDHANA'S HOUSE.

THE PAIN AND AGONY THAT TORTURED ME FOR FIVE LONG YEARS VANISHES WITH JUST ONE DOSE OF MEDICINE! I MUST BE DREAMING.

MAY THE CHILD WHO BROUGHT THIS DIVINE AUSHADHI* LIVE LONG!

WHEN THE CHILD HAD TO BE NAMED, SHRIVARDHANA MADE A DECISION.

IT IS A TRADITION IN OUR FAMILY FOR THE ELDEST SON TO BE NAMED AFTER HIS GRANDFATHER, BUT...

..., SINCE OUR SON WAS BORN WITH THE MIRACULOUS AUSHADHI, WE WILL BREAK THE TRADITION AND NAME HIM MAHAUSHADHA KUMAR.

* MEDICINE

MAHAUSHADHA KUMAR GREW UP HAPPILY IN THE COMPANY OF THE CHILDREN OF HIS VILLAGE. BUT HE WAS FAR MORE INTELLIGENT AND KNOWLEDGEABLE THAN ANY OF THEM. ONE DAY, WHEN HE WAS BARELY SEVEN YEARS OLD—

AUSHADHA, THE STREETS ARE TOO CROWDED. HOW CAN WE PLAY HERE? LET'S GO INDOORS.

BUT THE RAINS WILL SOON BE HERE AND THEN WE WILL HAVE TO PLAY INDOORS ALL THE TIME.

NO, WE WILL NOT. WE'LL HAVE A NEW TOWN WITH A SHELTERED PLAYGROUND. WE'LL ASK OUR PARENTS TO DONATE THE MONEY FOR IT.

AUSHADHA KUMAR ASSEMBLED ALL THE LOCAL ARTISANS AND SPOKE TO THEM OF HIS PLANS.

I WANT TO RAISE A TOWNSHIP WHICH WILL HAVE A STADIUM FOR CHILDREN, A HOME FOR HOMELESS WOMEN...

... REST-HOUSES FOR TRAVELLERS AND MENDICANTS, AND PUBLIC HALLS FOR PRAYERS AND SETTLING DISPUTES.

THE SIMPLE ARTISANS OF YAVAMAJJHAKA VILLAGE WERE UNABLE TO VISUALIZE AUSHADHA KUMAR'S IDEAS. SO HE MADE A PLAN OF THE TOWNSHIP FOR THEM. AND...

...WORK BEGAN AND PROGRESSED QUICKLY YET SMOOTHLY UNDER HIS SUPERVISION. AND...

...BEFORE LONG THE CHILDREN HAD AN EXCLUSIVE PLAYGROUND WITH SHELTERED SECTIONS WHERE THEY COULD PLAY WHEN IT RAINED. DESTITUTE WOMEN AND MENDICANTS AND TRAVELLERS ALIKE BLESSED THEIR BENEFACTOR, AUSHADHA KUMAR.

THE PEOPLE OF YAVAMAJJHAKA WERE SO IMPRESSED WITH AUSHADHA KUMAR THAT THEY OFTEN ASKED HIM TO SETTLE THEIR DISPUTES.

MEANWHILE, AS SEVERAL YEARS HAD PASSED SINCE THE ADVENT OF THE GREAT PANDIT WAS PREDICTED, KING VAIDEHA DECIDED TO SEEK HIM OUT.

MINISTERS, COMB THE WHOLE KINGDOM AND SEE IF YOU COME ACROSS ANY EXCEPTIONAL CHILD.

YES, MAHARAJ.

THE MINISTER WHO TRAVELLED EASTWARD...

...CAME TO YAVAMAJJHAKA.

WHO IS THE ARCHITECT OF THIS MAGNIFICENT TOWNSHIP?

AUSHADHA KUMAR, THE SON OF SETH SHRIVARDHANA.

HE MUST BE A VERY LEARNED MAN.

LEARNED HE CERTAINLY IS. BUT NOT YET A MAN. HE'S JUST A BOY OF SEVEN.

A BOY OF SEVEN? I MUST SEND A MESSAGE TO THE KING.

THE MINISTER'S MESSENGER SPED TO MITHILA.

MAHARAJ, THE MINISTER IS CONVINCED THAT SEVEN-YEAR-OLD AUSHADHA KUMAR OF YAVAMAJJHAKA IS THE CHILD YOU ARE LOOKING FOR.

I HAD MY DREAM ABOUT EIGHT YEARS AGO!

SENAK PANDIT, I THINK WE SHOULD INVITE AUSHADHA KUMAR TO MITHILA.

WHAT IF HE IS THE SOUL WHOSE WISDOM WILL SURPASS OUR KNOWLEDGE?

I AM NOT SO SURE, MAHARAJ. PLANNING A TOWNSHIP IS NO CRITERION OF WISDOM OR OF THE GREATNESS OF A SOUL.

YOU ARE RIGHT.

ASK THE MINISTER TO OBSERVE AUSHADHA KUMAR FOR A FEW MORE DAYS AND TO REPORT ANYTHING UNUSUAL HE SEES.

AS YOU COMMAND, MAHARAJ.

THE MINISTER DID AS HE WAS ORDERED. THEN ONE DAY—

HEY! THIEF! THIEF!

OH, GOD! WHAT SHALL I DO? A WHOLE LEG OF MUTTON GONE!

DON'T LOOK SO DEJECTED. I'LL GET IT BACK FOR YOU.

AUSHADHA KUMAR RUSHED LIKE THE WIND...

...TILL HE WAS RIGHT BELOW THE SHADOW OF THE FALCON. AND—

DROP THAT MEAT AT ONCE!

REPORT WHAT WE HAVE JUST SEEN TO THE KING.

SOON, AT MITHILA —

...AND, THE FALCON OBEYED HIM! MAHARAJ, THE MINISTER IS CONVINCED THAT AUSHADHA KUMAR IS ENDOWED WITH MYSTIC POWERS.

WELL, PANDIT SENAK? SHALL WE INVITE HIM HERE NOW?

HIS ARRIVAL WILL ROB US OF OUR STATUS. I MUST PREVENT HIS COMING HERE.

MAHARAJ, I AM STILL NOT CONVINCED. THE FALCON COULD HAVE DROPPED THE MEAT OUT OF SHEER FRIGHT.

SO THE MINISTER AT YAVAMAJJHAKA WAS ASKED TO CONTINUE HIS OBSERVATION OF AUSHADHA KUMAR.

12

ONE DAY—

EAT YOUR FILL, MY BEAUTIES.

MEANWHILE, I WILL REST HERE IN THE SHADE.

AS SOON AS THE OWNER OF THE BULLOCKS DOZED OFF—

WHAT MAGNIFICENT ANIMALS! THEY SHOULD FETCH AS MAGNIFICENT A PRICE.

ONE WHO SLEEPS IS ONE WHO LOSES.

HEY!

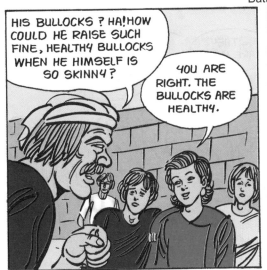

HIS BULLOCKS? HA! HOW COULD HE RAISE SUCH FINE, HEALTHY BULLOCKS WHEN HE HIMSELF IS SO SKINNY?

YOU ARE RIGHT. THE BULLOCKS ARE HEALTHY.

WHAT DO YOU FEED THEM TO MAKE THEM SO ROBUST?

OH, MASTER, I FEED THEM YAVAGU*, SESAMUM LADDOOS AND UDAD⊕!

AND YOU MY FRIEND, IF AS YOU CLAIM THESE ARE YOUR BULLOCKS, WHAT SPECIAL FEED DO YOU GIVE THEM?

I AM A POOR MAN. I CAN'T AFFORD SPECIAL FOOD. I FEED THEM ORDINARY HAY.

FRIENDS, GRIND A PASTE OF MUSTARD LEAVES AND FEED IT TO THE BULLOCKS.

* BARLEY GRUEL   ⊕ BLACK GRAM.

15

THE PASTE OF MUSTARD LEAVES HAD THE DESIRED LAXATIVE EFFECT.

NOW EXAMINE THE DUNG DROPPED BY THE BULLOCKS.

...DO YOU FIND ANY GRAINS OF BARLEY, SESAMUM OR UDAD?

NO! NOT A SINGLE ONE.

SO, YOU FEED YAVAGU AND UDAD TO THE BULLOCKS. DO YOU?

YOU ARE A THIEF!

Y-YES... I MEAN NO, MASTER.

NO... NO... YES...

ENRAGED BY SUCH RANK DECEIT, AUSHADHA KUMAR'S FRIENDS BEAT UP THE MAN.

THEN—

THE BULLOCKS ARE YOURS, FRIEND. YOU MAY LEAD THEM AWAY.

BUT WHEN THE TALE OF THE BULLOCKS WAS NARRATED IN THE COURT OF VAIDEHA —

MAHARAJ, ANYONE WITH COMMON SENSE CAN SOLVE SUCH A PROBLEM.

AND THE MINISTER WAS ASKED TO CONTINUE HIS VIGIL AT YAVAMAJJHAKA.

A FEW DAYS LATER, THE CASE OF AN OLD WOMAN WORKING IN A COTTON FIELD PRESENTED THE MINISTER WITH YET ANOTHER INSTANCE OF AUSHADHA KUMAR'S WISDOM.

HEY!•••

...WHAT ARE YOU DOING WITH MY YARN?

HA! YOUR YARN? WHO SAYS SO?

I SPUN IT. IT IS MY YARN. GIVE IT TO ME.

NOT ON YOUR LIFE! HAVE RUINED MY BEAUTIFUL, SOFT HANDS SPINNING THIS YARN. YOU ARE NOT GOING TO ROB ME OF IT.

THE TWO WOMEN WERE BROUGHT TO AUSHADHA KUMAR.

SO, BOTH OF YOU CLAIM THAT THE YARN IS YOURS.

YES!

YES!

THE EVER ALERT MINISTER WATCHED THE PROCCEDINGS.

AUSHADHA KUMAR STUDIED THE WOMEN CAREFULLY.

THE OLD WOMAN'S HANDS ARE ROUGH AND THERE ARE STRANDS OF COTTON IN HER HAIR...

...AND THIS WOMAN'S HANDS BETRAY THAT SHE BARELY DOES ANY HARD WORK.

WHAT HAVE YOU ROLLED THE YARN ON?

NOW THAT'S AN UNFAIR QUESTION. WHAT SHOULD I SAY?

MM-M-M... SINCE THE OLD WOMAN WORKS IN A COTTON FIELD SHE MUST HAVE USED A COTTON SEED...

IT'S ROLLED ON A COTTON SEED.

21

MOTHER IF IT IS YOUR YARN, WHAT HAVE YOU ROLLED IT ON?

ON A GOURD SEED, MASTER.

UNROLL THE THREAD.

IT IS A GOURD SEED.

HERE IS YOUR YARN, MOTHER. IT BELONGS TO YOU.

WHEN THE TALE REACHED MITHILA, THE PANDITS YET AGAIN REFUSED TO ADMIT THAT AUSHADHA KUMAR WAS ENDOWED WITH EXCEPTIONAL WISDOM.

THE PROBLEM OF THE YARN WAS SIMPLE. IT WOULD HAVE BEEN DIFFICULT IF...

...THE OLD WOMAN HAD USED A COTTON SEED.

THEREFORE IT CANNOT BE CONCLUDED THAT THIS BOY, AUSHADHA KUMAR IS IN ANY WAY GREAT.

IN THIS MANNER ON SEVEN OCCASIONS DID THE PANDITS OF MITHILA DISPUTE THE WISDOM OF AUSHADHA KUMAR TO STALL HIS INDUCTION INTO THE COURT. BUT VAIDEHA WAS TENACIOUS.

I SHALL TEST AUSHADHA KUMAR MYSELF.

HE HAD THE TAPERING STEM OF A SAPLING CUT AND SHAPED INTO A PERFECT CYLINDER.

GOOD! NOW NO ONE CAN TELL ONE END FROM THE OTHER.

THE PIECE OF WOOD WAS SENT TO SETH SHRIVARDHANA'S HOUSE.

KING VAIDEHA WANTS THE SHOOT END AND THE ROOT END OF THIS STEM TO BE IDENTIFIED.

BOTH ENDS LOOK THE SAME. HOW CAN ONE TELL WHICH IS WHICH?

LET ME TRY.

IN A PLANT, THE ROOT END IS HEAVIER THAN THE SHOOT END.

SO THE END THAT DIPS INTO THE WATER IS THE ROOT END AND THE OTHER, OF COURSE, THE SHOOT END.

WHILE THE FOUR PANDITS WERE DOWNCAST BY THE RESULTS OF THE FIRST TEST, THE KING WAS DELIGHTED. AUSHADHA HAD WON THE FIRST ROUND WITH FULL MARKS.

HE IS CERTAINLY KNOWLEDGEABLE AND OBSERVANT. NOW LET ME SEE IF HE IS CLEVER AND HAS HIS WITS ABOUT HIM.

AND SO— THE KING WANTS YOU TO SEND HIM A ROPE, AS THE ROPE OF HIS SWING SUDDENLY SNAPPED.

WE SHALL BE HONOURED TO BE OF SERVICE TO OUR KING.

I AM SURE YOU WOULD, BUT HIS ROPE WAS NOT AN ORDINARY ONE.

IT WAS MADE OF SAND. AND HE WANTS AN IDENTICAL ONE.

BUT HOW CAN ONE MAKE A ROPE OF SAND?

I KNOW HOW. BUT I HAVE A SMALL PROBLEM.

... I DO NOT KNOW HOW THICK THE SNAPPED ROPE WAS.

IF HE COULD PROVIDE US WITH A SAMPLE, WE'LL MAKE AN IDENTICAL ONE FOR HIM.

WHEN THE KING HEARD THE COUNTER DEMAND—

REMARKABLE! THE BOY IS EXTRAORDINARY!

KING VAIDEHA POSED SEVERAL SUCH COMPLEX PROBLEMS WHICH PUT AUSHADHA KUMAR'S WITS SEVERELY TO THE TEST. FINALLY—

AUSHADHA KUMAR IS BEYOND DOUBT A GREAT SOUL I SHALL NOW INVITE HIM TO JOIN MY COURT.

BUT, MAHARAJ...

NOW I SHALL GO AND FETCH THE GREAT PANDIT HERE MYSELF.

NEXT MORNING, THE KING LEFT HIS CAPITAL FOR YAVAMAJJHAKA.

HOWEVER ON THE WAY—

THE HORSE HAS BROKEN ITS LEG.

THIS IS A BAD OMEN, MAHARAJ. YOU SHOULD GIVE UP THE IDEA OF MEETING AUSHADHA KUMAR.

IT IS NOT A BAD OMEN. THE HORSE TRIPPED. I WILL NOT BE DETERRED FROM MEETING AUSHADHA KUMAR JUST BECAUSE OF AN ACCIDENT.

BUT HOW WILL YOU TRAVEL NOW? YOUR ROYAL MOUNT IS INJURED. LET US RETURN TO THE CAPITAL AND SEND ANOTHER CRYPTIC MESSAGE TO AUSHADHA KUMAR. LET US SEE IF HE STANDS THIS FINAL TEST.

SOON—

THE ROYAL HORSE IS INJURED, SETH SHRIVARDHANA. PLEASE SEND A MULE OR ITS SUPERIOR FOR THE KING.

WHAT KIND OF A DEMAND IS THIS? A MULE OR ITS SUPERIOR!! SHALL WE SEND A DONKEY WHICH IS SUPERIOR TO THE MULE BY VIRTUE OF BEING ITS FATHER?

FATHER, IT IS NEITHER MULE NOR DONKEY THAT THE KING WANTS, BUT YOU AND ME.

I MUST PUT AN END TO THIS BATTLE OF WITS.

HOW WILL YOU DO THAT SON?

BY SHOWING DISRESPECT TO YOU IN THE COURT, FATHER.

BUT SON,... YOU HAVE ALWAYS RESPECTED ME.

AND I ALWAYS WILL, FATHER. WHAT I AM GOING TO DO IS ONLY A PART OF A SCHEME.

YOU GO TO THE COURT FIRST. I WILL FOLLOW YOU.

WHEN THE KING ASKS ME TO TAKE A SEAT, YOU GET UP AND I WILL SIT IN YOUR PLACE.

ALL RIGHT, SON.

WHEN SETH SHRIVARDHANA REACHED THE COURT—

GLORY TO KING VAIDEHA.

WHERE IS YOUR SON?

HE IS ON HIS WAY, MAHARAJ.

AS ARRANGED, AUSHADHA KUMAR FOLLOWED HIS FATHER TO MITHILA.

WHEN AUSHADHA KUMAR REACHED THE COURT —

SALUTATIONS, MAHARAJ.

PLEASE CHOOSE A SEAT THAT BEFITS YOUR STATUS, O PANDIT.

AS YOU COMMAND, MAHARAJ.

LOOK AT HIM!

AUSHADHA KUMAR HAS NO RESPECT FOR HIS FATHER. AND HE CALLS HIMSELF A PANDIT. IN FACT HE IS NO BETTER THAN THE DONKEY HE HAS BROUGHT WITH HIM.

HA! HA! HO! HO!

HA! HA! HA! HEE! HEE!

HA! HA HEE! HEE HEE HA! HEE

YOU LOOK UNHAPPY, MAHARAJ.

I NEVER DREAMT THAT ONE WHOM I HAD HELD IN SUCH HIGH ESTEEM WOULD LET ME DOWN SO BADLY.

HOW COULD YOU MAKE YOUR FATHER GET UP AND OCCUPY HIS SEAT!

DO YOU ALWAYS CONSIDER THE FATHER TO BE SUPERIOR TO THE SON?

ALWAYS!

WHO IS SUPERIOR? A DONKEY OR A MULE?

THE MULE, OF COURSE.

BUT THE DONKEY IS THE FATHER OF THE MULE.

I KNOW, BUT THE MULE IS A BETTER ANIMAL. IT IS STURDIER AND CAPABLE OF HARDER WORK.

AND SO IT SOMETIMES IS WITH MAN. A YOUNG PERSON CAN SOMETIMES BE WISER THAN HIS ELDERS.

AND ONE, TO WHOM THE WELFARE OF THE STATE IS ENTRUSTED, SHOULD SELECT HIS COUNSELLORS GUIDED BY THIS FACT.

SETH SHRIVARDHANA, I WISH TO ADOPT AUSHADHA KUMAR AS MY SON. DO I HAVE YOUR PERMISSION?

YOU DO, MAHARAJ. IT WOULD BE SELFISH OF ME TO REFUSE WHEN THE PEOPLE AND THE STATE WOULD BENIFIT SO GREATLY BY THIS ADOPTION.

I GRANT YOU THE VILLAGE OF YAVAMAJJHAKA IN APPRECIATION OF YOUR SELFLESS GESTURE, SETH SHRIVARDHANA.

SETH SHRIVARDHANA RETURNED TO YAVAMAJJHAKA AND AUSHADHA KUMAR WAS FORMALLY ADOPTED BY KING VAIDEHA OF MITHILA.

TRUE FRIENDS

JATAKA TALES OF GOOD CONDUCT

The route to your roots

TRUE FRIENDS

Friends are our most valuable possession – that is the lesson these Jataka tales impart. The wise, like Nigrodha Kumar, cherish their companions. Pottik's selfless loyalty is rewarded by unexpected riches. On the other hand, for the selfish ingrate Shakha there awaits only a shameful loneliness. Rich or poor, ugly or handsome, powerful or helpless, a friend is one whom you can trust. And for this luxury, you should repay your friend with respect and honour.

Script	Illustrations	Editor
Margie Sastry	V.B.Halbe	Anant Pai

Cover illustration by: C.D.Rane

TRUE FRIENDS

LONG LONG AGO, DURING THE REIGN OF KING MAGADHA, A WEDDING WAS BEING CELEBRATED IN RAJAGRIHA.

WHAT A SUMPTUOUS FEAST!

AND SUCH POMP AND CEREMONY!

AND WHY NOT? AFTER ALL THE GROOM'S FATHER IS THE RICHEST MERCHANT IN TOWN.

THE BRIDE WAS DEMURE AND BEAUTIFUL.

HOW LOVELY SHE LOOKS!

THE SETH OF JANAPAD HAS GIVEN SUCH GENEROUS GIFTS TO HIS DAUGHTER.

AT FIRST, THE BRIDE WAS TREATED WITH TENDERNESS.

NO! DON'T DO ANY WORK. YOUR LOVELY HANDS WILL BE SPOILT.

BUT A FEW MONTHS LATER—

DON'T SIT THERE DREAMING. CAN'T YOU LEND A HAND IN THE HOUSEWORK?

1

NO BUTS! JUST DO AS I SAY!

WHY HAS SHE CHANGED TOWARDS ME? WHAT HAVE I DONE?

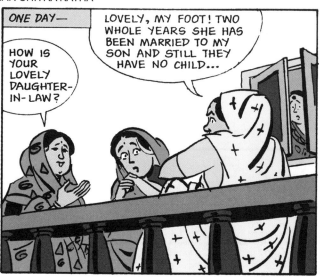

ONE DAY—

HOW IS YOUR LOVELY DAUGHTER-IN-LAW?

LOVELY, MY FOOT! TWO WHOLE YEARS SHE HAS BEEN MARRIED TO MY SON AND STILL THEY HAVE NO CHILD...

AFTER ALL WE MUST HAVE AN HEIR TO CARRY ON THE FAMILY NAME.

HMM! SO THAT'S IT!

THE WORRIED DAUGHTER-IN-LAW CONFIDED IN HER MAID.

I WILL NOT GET ANY RESPECT IN THIS HOUSE UNLESS I AM WITH CHILD

WHY DON'T YOU PRETEND TO BE SO?

WITH THE ADVICE AND HELP OF THE MAID, THE DAUGHTER-IN-LAW PRETENDED TO BE AN EXPECTANT MOTHER AND ONCE AGAIN SHE BEGAN TO BE FUSSED OVER.

HERE! I'VE MADE A SPECIAL SWEET FOR YOU.

IN DUE COURSE—

I THINK IT'S TIME TO GO TO MY PARENTS' HOUSE.

YES, BY TRADITION YOU MUST GO THERE FOR YOUR DELIVERY.

SHE SET OUT ON HER JOURNEY WITH HER PERSONAL MAID AND AN ATTENDANT.

THERE'S A CARAVAN AHEAD OF US!

LET'S TRY TO GO WITH THEM.

YES, IT IS SAFER TO TRAVEL WITH A GROUP.

THEY ACCOMPANIED THE CARAVAN WHICH CAMPED IN THE EVENING NEAR A GROVE OF TREES.

NEXT MORNING—

OH! THE CARAVAN HAS MOVED ON!

WHAT'S THIS? A NEW-BORN BABY!

SEE THERE!

WHAT! OH! THE CARVAN PEOPLE MUST HAVE ABANDONED IT!

ARE YOU THINKING WHAT I'M THINKING?

YES! LET'S PRETEND IT IS YOUR BABY.

WAKE UP! OUR LADY HAS GIVEN BIRTH TO A BABY BOY.

WHAT? ALREADY?

HURRY UP AND GIVE THE GOOD NEWS TO HER HUSBAND AND FAMILY.

TAKE ONE OF THE HORSES.

BY AFTERNOON THE ATTENDANT GALLOPED BACK.

I RUSHED BACK TO TELL YOU.

(HUFF PUFF)

YOUR PARENTS-IN-LAW WANT YOU TO GO BACK.

YES, THERE'S NO POINT IN GOING TO MY PARENTS' HOUSE NOW.

THEY RETURNED TO RAJAGRIHA AMIDST A JOYOUS WELCOME.

AN HEIR AT LAST!

WHAT A LOVELY BOY! WE MUST CELEBRATE HIS BIRTH WITH GREAT POMP.

AT THE NAMING CEREMONY —

SINCE THE BOY WAS BORN UNDER A NIGRODHA* TREE, WE SHALL CALL HIM NIGRODHA KUMAR.

JUST THEN —

OH, SIR, TWO MORE BOYS WERE BORN IN OUR CITY ON THE SAME DAY AS OUR YOUNG MASTER.

IN WHICH HOUSE?

IN THE WEAVER'S HOUSE THERE IS A NEW-BORN WHO IS NAMED POTTIK.

AND IN THE MERCHANTS HOUSE, THE BOY HAS BEEN NAMED SHAKHA KUMAR.

LET THEM BE BROUGHT HERE! THEY WILL BE GOOD COMPANY FOR MY SON.

* NYAGRODHA (SANSK): BANYAN

5

THE THREE BOYS PLAYED TOGETHER ALL DAY.

NOW IT'S MY TURN, POTTIK!

AND AFTER YOU, NIGRODHA KUMAR, YOU MUST GIVE A CHANCE TO SHAKHA.

EVEN AS A CHILD, POTTIK SHOWED A SENSE OF FAIR PLAY.

WHEN THEY WERE ABOUT ELEVEN YEARS OLD—

WE MUST GO TO TAKSHASHILA FOR STUDIES.

YOU TWO CAN AFFORD THE TWO THOUSAND -COIN FEE...

... BUT MY POOR FATHER IS JUST A WEAVER. I CANNOT GO WITH YOU.

YES, YOU CAN.

I SPOKE TO MY FATHER AND HE HAS AGREED TO PAY FOR YOUR STUDIES TOO.

HOW GOOD OF HIM.

WHILE STUDYING TOGETHER AT TAKSHASHILA—

HOW TIME HAS FLOWN!

OUR STUDIES ARE OVER!

WE CAN GO HOME.

NO! I THINK WE SHOULD TRAVEL A WHILE.

HMM... A GOOD IDEA!

YES, TRAVEL WILL BROADEN OUR MINDS.

WHILE ROAMING FROM ONE PLACE TO ANOTHER, THEY REACHED THE OUTSKIRTS OF VARANASI.

LET'S REST HERE FOR A WHILE UNDER THE TREES.

THEY SPENT THE NIGHT THERE. EARLY AT DAWN, POTTIK WOKE UP AFTER HEARING THE CACKLE OF A HEN.

CACKLE

WHY ARE YOU CACKLING SO LOUDLY OVER AN EGG?

BECAUSE THIS ONE IS NOT AN ORDINARY EGG. THE ONE WHO EATS THE YOLK OF IT IS DESTINED TO BE A KING...

... THE ONE WHO EATS THE WHITE OF IT WILL BECOME COMMANDER OF THE ARMY...

... AND THE ONE WHO EATS THE SHELL WILL BECOME A TREASURER. WELL, ISN'T SUCH AN EGG WORTH CROWING ABOUT?

YES, I AGREE.

I MUST TRY TO FIND OUT WHETHER THERE IS ANY TRUTH IN WHAT THE HEN SAID.

WHEN THE HENS MOVED AWAY, POTTIK QUIETLY PICKED UP THE EGG.

LET'S TRY OUR LUCK.

CAREFULLY HE SEPARATED THE PARTS OF THE EGG AND MIXED THEM IN THE BREAKFAST PORRIDGE.

HERE'S YOUR PORRIDGE, NIGRODHA.

WITH THE YOLK.

AND THIS IS YOURS, SHAKHA.

THE WHITE IS IN THIS ONE.

I'LL EAT THE ONE WITH THE SHELL.

WHEN THEY HAD FINISHED EATING—

NOW IF WHAT THE HEN SAID IS TRUE, YOU WILL BECOME A KING SOON, NIGRODHA. SHAKHA WILL BECOME THE COMMANDER OF THE ARMY AND I THE TREASURER.

WHAT DO YOU MEAN?

I HEARD THE HEN THAT LAID THIS EGG SAY TO ANOTHER HEN THAT THIS EGG HAS MIRACULOUS EFFECTS.

POTTIK REPEATED WHAT HE HAD HEARD.

BUT WE HAVEN'T EATEN ANY PART OF THE EGG.

YES, YOU HAVE. I SEPARATED THE PARTS AND SERVED THEM TO EACH OF YOU.

I GAVE THE YOLK TO NIGRODHA, THE WHITE TO SHAKHA AND I ATE THE SHELL MYSELF.

SHAKHA WAS UNHAPPY BUT KEPT SILENT.

WHO IS HE TO DECIDE? HE SHOULD HAVE GIVEN THE YOLK TO ME. I'LL TEACH HIM A LESSON ONE DAY.

HE PRETENDED THAT HE WAS NOT HURT.

WELL, LET'S SEE WHAT THE FUTURE BRINGS US.

LET'S GO INTO THE TOWN OF VARANASI.

THEY WERE WARMLY WELCOMED AT THE FIRST HOUSE THEY VISITED.

IT'S MY LUCKY DAY TO HAVE GUESTS LIKE YOU EARLY IN THE MORNING.

IT'S BEEN SEVEN DAYS SINCE OUR CHILDLESS KING DIED.

NOW WHO WILL RULE HERE?

DON'T YOU KNOW THE TRADITION? A FLOWER-DECORATED CHARIOT WILL BE SENT OUT TODAY. IT WILL HAVE NO CHARIOTEER. BUT THE NEW KING WILL BE THE ONE IN FRONT OF WHOM THE CHARIOT STOPS.

THE THREE YOUNG MEN THANKED THEIR HOST FOR THE MEAL AND SET OUT. AFTER ROAMING FOR A WHILE—

LET'S REST IN THE PARK.

IT'S COOL THERE.

NIGRODHA KUMAR SLEPT ON A STONE-SLAB IN THE PARK.

THE OTHER TWO SLEPT ON THE BROAD STEPS OUTSIDE THE PARK.

THEY DID NOT EVEN HEAR THE APPROACHING HUBBUB.

HURRAY! THE FLORAL CHARIOT IS HERE!

LET'S FOLLOW IT AND SEE WHERE IT STOPS.

AN EXCITED MOB FOLLOWED THE DECORATED CHARIOT.

AT THE ENTRANCE OF THE PARK—

LOOK! THE HORSE WANTS TO ASCEND THOSE STEPS.

THE HORSE HAS STOPPED!

THERE MUST BE SOME WORTHY SOUL IN THE PARK. LET ME SEE.

AH! WHAT A NOBLE FACE THIS YOUNG MAN HAS.

THE PRIEST REMOVED THE CLOTH COVERING NIGRODHA'S FEET.

HIS FEET HAVE THE SIGNS OF AN EMPEROR.

HUH WHAT'S THIS? CAN'T YOU LET A FELLOW SLEEP?

HE TURNED OVER AND TRIED TO GO BACK TO SLEEP.

SEE HIS FACE.

AND HIS FEET.

THE HUBBUB BY THEN HAD TURNED INTO AN UPROAR.

AH WELL! I MIGHT AS WELL GET UP.

WHISPER WHISPER

OH, SIRE! YOU ARE OUR CHOSEN KING. ACCEPT THIS CROWN AND THE KINGDOM.

BUT WHY ME?

OUR FLORAL CHARIOT LOCATED YOU AND I FOUND ALL THE ROYAL SIGNS ON YOUR PERSON. YOU SHALL BE OUR KING.

SO BE IT.

NIGRODHA KUMAR WAS PROMPTLY INSTALLED AS THE KING.

I NAME SHAKHA KUMAR AS MY COMMANDER-IN-CHIEF.

POTTIK, YOU MUST STAY WITH ME AS MY CONSTANT COMPANION.

VERY WELL, O KING!

THE THREE FRIENDS BEGAN TO LIVE IN LUXURY IN THE PALACE. ONE DAY—

I MISS MY FATHER AND MOTHER.

HE TURNED TO SHAKHA—

WILL YOU GO AND FETCH THEM HERE?

NO, I CANNOT LEAVE MY SOLDIERS NOW. I'M NEEDED HERE.

WILL YOU GO POTTIK?

OF COURSE I WILL.

WITH A SMALL RETINUE, POTTIK SOON SET OFF.

IN A FEW DAYS HE REACHED RAJAGRIHA AND THEN NIGRODHA KUMAR'S HOUSE.

YOUR SON HAS BECOME A KING, HE HAS SENT ME TO FETCH YOU.

WE ARE HAPPY FOR HIM.

BUT I CANNOT LEAVE MY BUSINESS HERE.

AND WE DON'T WANT TO GO AWAY FROM OUR OWN HOUSE TO A FAR OFF PLACE.

GIVE HIM OUR BLESSINGS AND TELL HIM WE ARE WELL AND HAPPY.

AS YOU WISH.

HE REQUESTED SHAKHA KUMAR'S PARENTS.

TELL HIM HOW PROUD WE ARE OF HIM. BUT WE CANNOT LEAVE OUR ANCESTRAL HOME.

POTTIK THEN WENT TO HIS OWN HOUSE.

COME WITH ME TO VARANASI.

NO, SON! OUR PLACE IS HERE.

WE CANNOT COME WITH YOU.

WITH A HEAVY HEART POTTIK RETURNED TO VARANASI.

OH! WHAT A JOURNEY. I AM SO TIRED.

POTTIK HAD SPENT ALL HIS MONEY BY THEN.

HERE'S SHAKHA'S HOUSE. I'LL REST HERE AND REFRESH MYSELF BEFORE GOING TO THE PALACE.

TELL YOUR MASTER THAT HIS FRIEND POTTIK IS HERE.

SIR, YOUR FRIEND POTTIK IS HERE.

AH! NOW'S MY CHANCE TO TAKE REVENGE!

HAD HE GIVEN ME THE YOLK, I WOULD HAVE BECOME THE KING.

15

WHO'S POTTIK? I DON'T KNOW ANYONE BY THAT NAME. BEAT HIM AND THROW HIM OUT. HE MUST BE A MADCAP.

OUR MASTER TOLD US TO THROW YOU OUT.

HUH?

WHAT AN UNGRATEFUL WRETCH. IT IS BECAUSE OF ME THAT HE HAS SO MANY SOLDIERS AT HIS COMMAND. AND NOW HE TELLS THEM TO THROW ME OUT.

I'M SURE MY FRIEND NIGRODHA WILL NOT BEHAVE THUS.

POTTIK REACHED THE PALACE, LATE IN THE EVENING —

O KING! YOUR FRIEND POTTIK DESIRES TO SEE YOU.

BRING HIM IN RIGHT AWAY.

16

COME, YOU MUST BE TIRED AFTER YOUR JOURNEY.

MINISTER! CALL FOR THE ROYAL BARBER. LET HIM ATTEND TO MY DEAR FRIEND. ARRANGE FOR A BATH, FRESH CLOTHES AND ORNAMENTS. WE WILL EAT OUR FOOD TOGETHER.

HOW WAS YOUR JOURNEY? DID YOU MEET MY PARENTS?

YES, BUT I COULDN'T PERSUADE THEM TO COME.

AH! WELL! MAY BE THEY ARE HAPPIER AT RAJAGRIHA.

I THOUGHT SO TOO.

JUST THEN SHAKHA ARRIVED.

OH! THAT POTTIK IS WITH THE KING. HE WILL SURELY TELL TALES. PERHAPS HE MAY NOT DARE TO SAY THINGS AGAINST ME IN MY PRESENCE.

AH! SHAKHA! SEE POTTIK IS BACK FROM RAJAGRIHA!

OH, BUT SHAKHA DOESN'T KNOW ME.

WHAT?

REALLY, I STOPPED BY AT HIS HOUSE ON MY WAY HERE, BUT HE SAID HE DIDN'T KNOW ME AND HAD ME BEATEN AND THROWN OUT BY HIS GUARDS.

HOW COULD HE DO THAT? WE BOTH OWE OUR WEALTH AND STATUS TO YOU. AFTER ALL YOU COULD HAVE CHOSEN TO BE THE KING YOURSELF.

INDEED, ANY FAVOUR DONE TO AN UNGRATEFUL MAN IS LIKE A SEED BURNT BY FIRE. NOTHING EVER COMES OUT OF IT.

A FAVOUR DONE TO A DESERVING NOBLE PERSON IS LIKE A SEED SOWN IN FERTILE SOIL. IT WILL REAP RICH REWARDS.

HE TURNED TO SHAKHA—

DO YOU KNOW POTTIK?

SHAKHA'S SILENCE INFURIATED THE KING.

O YOU WICKED LIAR! TAKE HIM AWAY! KILL HIM.

POTTIK INTERVENED—

NO! PLEASE DON'T, O KING! IT IS NOT EASY TO BRING ANYONE BACK TO LIFE...

THEREFORE, I DON'T WANT HIM KILLED. PLEASE FORGIVE HIM.

IF YOU INSIST. BUT I WANT HIM BANISHED FROM MY KINGDOM.

NOW, I WANT YOU TO BE MY COMMANDER-IN-CHIEF, POTTIK.

THANK YOU.

BUT I MUST REFUSE. I HAVE ALWAYS KNOWN MY LIMITATIONS.

BUT YOU MUST ACCEPT SOME POSITION IN MY COURT.

WHY DON'T YOU ACCEPT THE POST OF BHANDAGARIK IN MY COURT?

WHAT ARE THE RESPONSI-BILITIES?

YOU WILL HAVE THE AUTHORITY TO DETERMINE THE TAXES PAYABLE BY THE MEMBERS OF THE VARIOUS GUILDS. YOU WILL BE IN CHARGE OF THE TREASURY.

AS YOU WISH. I ACCEPT THE POST.

WITH POTTIK BY HIS SIDE NIGRODHA KUMAR RULED WISELY AND WELL FOR MANY YEARS.

KANNI, THE UNLUCKY *

DURING THE REIGN OF BRAHMADATTA IN VARANASI, THERE LIVED A PROSPEROUS MERCHANT CALLED ANATHAPINDIKA.

ONE DAY—

SIR! A MAN CALLED KALAKANNI ** IS HERE TO SEE YOU!

SHOW HIM IN!

BUT, SIR! HE LOOKS VERY POOR AND WRETCHED!

NEVER MIND! IT MUST BE MY OLD FRIEND. AFTER ALL, NOT MANY PEOPLE HAVE A NAME LIKE HIS!

AS YOU WISH, SIR.

KALAKANNI WALKED IN HESITANTLY.

AH! IT IS YOU. HOW GOOD TO MEET YOU AFTER ALL THESE YEARS!

YES! IT IS.

* BASED ON KALAKANNI JATAKA ** UNLUCKY

20

BUT WHY DO YOU LOOK SO DOWN AND OUT?

MY LUCK, I GUESS. WHOEVER CHOSE MY NAME WAS RIGHT. I AM REALLY UNLUCKY.

HUSH! DON'T EVER SAY THAT!

BUT, TRULY, I HAVE BEEN SO MISERABLE.

NOT ANY MORE! NOW YOU WILL STAY WITH ME AND SHARE MY LIFE.

BUT...

NO BUTS! I WILL NOT LET YOU GO. AFTER ALL HOW CAN I EVER FORGET A FRIEND LIKE YOU?

YES! THOSE DAYS WE SPENT TOGETHER AT THE GURUKULA* WERE THE HAPPIEST OF MY LIFE.

I HAVE A BIG BUSINESS HERE. I NEED A TRUSTWORTHY FRIEND LIKE YOU TO HELP ME.

WELL, I WILL STAY IF I CAN BE OF ANY USE.

KALAKANNI HELPED ANATHAPINDIKA IN HIS WORK.

* HERMITAGE OF THE GURU.

21

HE WAS TREATED LIKE A MEMBER OF THE FAMILY.

KALAKANNI! COME FOR LUNCH.

AFFECTIONATELY HE WAS CALLED KANNI.

KANNI! TAKE THESE MOHURS AND KEEP THEM SAFELY.

ANATHAPINDIKA'S BUSINESS ASSOCIATES WERE PERPLEXED.

HOW CAN YOU TRUST A STRANGER SO MUCH?

HE IS NO STRANGER! HE IS MY CHILDHOOD FRIEND.

BUT YOU HAVE NOT SEEN HIM FOR YEARS!

AND WHAT AN INAUSPICIOUS NAME— KALAKANNI.

WHY, EVEN UTTERING SUCH A NAME REPEATEDLY MIGHT BRING YOU BAD LUCK.

BAH! I DON'T BELIEVE IN SUCH THINGS.

THEY SAY THAT A MAN WHO WALKS SEVEN STEPS WITH YOU BECOMES A FRIEND. AFTER A FORTNIGHT OF BEING TOGETHER, HE IS LIKE A FAMILY MEMBER...

... I HAD SPENT YEARS WITH KALAKANNI IN THE GURUKULA.

AND HE IS A REAL GEM, WHATEVER BE HIS NAME.

I DON'T KNOW HOW YOU CAN STAND TO SEE SUCH AN UGLY MAN ALL DAY.

IF I WERE IN YOUR PLACE I WOULD GET RID OF HIM.

WELL! YOU ARE NOT IN MY PLACE.

AND HE IS HERE FOR GOOD.

AFTER A FEW MONTHS—

I'LL BE AWAY FOR A FEW DAYS. WE ARE GOING TO OUR NATIVE PLACE FOR A WEDDING.

BUT WHO WILL LOOK AFTER YOUR HOUSE?

OH! KALAKANNI WILL BE THERE.

YOU MEAN YOU WILL TRUST HIM WITH ALL YOUR VALUABLE BELONGINGS?

I CAN TRUST HIM WITH MY LIFE.

HERE ARE THE KEYS! KALAKANNI! TAKE CARE.

YOU MUST PLAY ON THE DRUM.

YOU HAVE A SWEET VOICE, YOU MUST SING.

THE REST OF US WILL CLAP WITH THE RHYTHM. MAKE AS MUCH NOISE AS YOU CAN.

AT NIGHT—

COME, LET'S ENTER THE EMPTY HOUSE.

WHEN THE DACOITS ARRIVED—

AAA

THUMP! THUMP!

YOU SAID IT WAS EMPTY!

IT SOUNDS AS IF THERE'S A CELEBRATION GOING ON.

WHY, THERE MUST BE A REAL CROWD INSIDE.

CLAP CLAP

THE SETH MUST HAVE RETURNED.

26

A MONK IN NEED* IS A FRIEND INDEED

ONE DAY KING BRAHMA-DATTA OF VARANASI AND HIS SON WERE BUSY DISCUSSING MATTERS OF STATE.

WE MUST SEND MORE SOLDIERS OF OUR ARMY TO THE PROVINCES.

YES, I HAVE DISCUSSED RECRUITING NEW SOLDIERS WITH THE COMMANDER.

JUST THEN—

OH! THAT IS THE MONK TIRITAVACHCHHA! I MUST GO AND RECEIVE HIM.

BUT, FATHER, YOU DON'T NEED TO GO. HE'LL BE GIVEN ALMS LIKE THE OTHER MONKS.

BUT THE KING RUSHED OUT TO WELCOME THE MONK.

COME, YOU MUST SIT HERE.

ON THE THRONE?

HOW ODD!

SOON—

YOUR MAJESTY, THE LUNCH HAS BEEN SERVED FOR ROYAL GUESTS. SHALL I TAKE YOUR GUEST THERE?

NO. HE WILL EAT WITH ME HERE IN MY PRIVATE CHAMBER.

AFTER LUNCH, THE CHIEF MINISTER WAS SUMMONED.

SEND FOR THE ARCHITECT. I WANT HIM TO BUILD A SUITABLE DWELLING FOR TIRITAVACHCHHA IN THE COMPOUND. IT SHOULD BE SPACIOUS AND COMFORTABLE.

AS YOU WISH, YOUR MAJESTY.

THE SPECIAL TREATMENT GIVEN TO TIRITAVACHCHHA DID NOT GO UNNOTICED.

WHAT A FUSS OVER AN ORDINARY MONK.

OUR KING TREATS HIM AS IF HE WERE A BRAVE WARRIOR WHO HAS MADE A GREAT CONQUEST.

* BASED ON TIRITAVACHCHHA JATAKA.

27

SOON IT REACHED THE PRINCE'S EARS.

FATHER, WHY DO YOU GIVE THIS MAN SO MUCH IMPORTANCE?

HE IS NOT AN EXPERT IN ANY ART. HE IS NEITHER YOUR RELATIVE NOR YOUR FRIEND.

HOW COME HE DESERVES SUCH ROYAL TREATMENT?

DO YOU REMEMBER, SON, TWO MONTHS AGO, I WENT WITH THE ARMY TO QUELL A REBELLION IN THE DISTRICTS?

" WHILE LEADING OUR SOLDIERS, MY ELEPHANT RAN IN A FRENZY AND WENT INTO THE FOREST. I WAS WOUNDED AND TIRED. LUCKILY WE REACHED AN ASHRAMA.

A WELL AT LAST. AH! I MUST HAVE SOME WATER!

BUT THERE WAS NO PULLEY TO DRAW THE WATER NOR ANYONE AROUND TO HELP.

I'LL TIE THE ROPE AROUND THE ELEPHANT'S LEG AND CLIMB DOWN THE WELL.

" I CLIMBED DOWN THE WELL AND DRANK MY FILL OF COOL WATER.

BUT THEN —

IT'S TOO SLIPPERY. I CAN'T GO BACK.

"IN THE EVENING. THE MONK TIRITAVACHCHHA RETURNED TO HIS ASHRAMA

AN ELEPHANT HERE! SURELY THERE MUST BE A RIDER TOO.

"THE MONK LOOKED AROUND —

AH! THERE YOU ARE·WAIT! I'LL HELP YOU OUT.

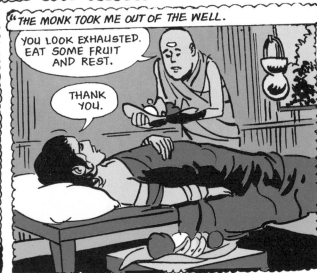

"THE MONK TOOK ME OUT OF THE WELL.

YOU LOOK EXHAUSTED. EAT SOME FRUIT AND REST.

THANK YOU.

"FOR TWO DAYS THE MONK LOOKED AFTER ME TREATING MY WOUNDS WITH HERBS AND BRINGING FOOD FOR ME FROM THE FOREST.

YOU HAVE SAVED MY LIFE! YOU MUST COME AND VISIT ME IN VARANASI.

HAD HE NOT RESCUED ME AND LOOKED AFTER ME, I WOULD NOT HAVE SURVIVED.

YES, FATHER, NOW I UNDERSTAND THAT YOU OWE YOUR LIFE TO HIM.

DON'T YOU THINK HE DESERVES TO BE MY FRIEND?

INDEED, FATHER. WE MUST DO ALL WE CAN FOR HIM.

Suppandi and his friends are all packed!

THE HIDDEN TREASURE

WISDOM WINS A WAR

The route to your roots

THE HIDDEN TREASURE

Mahajanaka was all set to wage a bloody war. Fate, however, had other plans. It turned his battlefield into a magnificent palace, where he was required to woo and win a beautiful princess. Wit was to be his most valuable weapon. Strong, handsome and yet wise, such a battle was easy for the young man. But for the many others who coveted his throne, it was an insurmountable hurdle.

Script
Meera Ugra

Illustrations
M.N.Nangare

Editor
Anant Pai

THE HIDDEN TREASURE

ONE DAY, LONG LONG AGO, A WOMAN CAME WALKING DEJECTEDLY DOWN THE ROAD THAT LED AWAY FROM THE CITY OF MITHILA. HER STEPS WERE SLOW AND HER FEET DRAGGED.

SHE WORE THE GARB OF A MAID BUT SEEMED TO BE OF NOBLE BIRTH.

I CANNOT WALK A STEP FARTHER. WHAT SHALL I DO? PERHAPS THAT CARTER WILL...

HOW FAR ARE YOU GOING, SIR? CAN YOU TAKE ME TO KALACHAMPA?

SHE LOOKS TIRED AND MISERABLE, POOR THING.

I'LL TAKE YOU THERE. PLEASE GET INTO MY CART.

YOU ARE VERY KIND, SIR! I...I DON'T KNOW HOW TO THANK YOU.

1

I CANNOT BELIEVE MY GOOD LUCK. THE GODS ARE WITH ME, TO BE SURE!

AS THE CART JOGGED ALONG, THE EXHAUSTED WOMAN FELL ASLEEP.

WHEN SHE WOKE UP IT WAS EVENING.

WHICH CITY IS THIS?

WHY, IT'S THE CITY OF KALACHAMPA! WE HAVE ARRIVED.

HE BROUGHT HIS CART TO A HALT AT THE SOUTHERN GATE OF THE CITY.

IT WILL BE EASIER FOR YOU TO ENTER THE CITY FROM HERE.

I AM GRATEFUL TO YOU FOR BRINGING ME HERE, KIND SIR.

AFTER ALIGHTING FROM THE CART...

...SHE WALKED INTO THE CITY.

I CAME HERE BECAUSE THIS WAS THE ONLY CITY I'D HEARD OF. WHERE SHALL I GO NOW?

A LITTLE LATER, A TEACHER CAME BY WITH HIS PUPILS.

SURPRISED TO SEE A WOMAN SITTING THERE ALONE, HE WALKED UP TO HER.

WHO ARE YOU? YOU SEEM TO BE IN DISTRESS.

I...I AM...

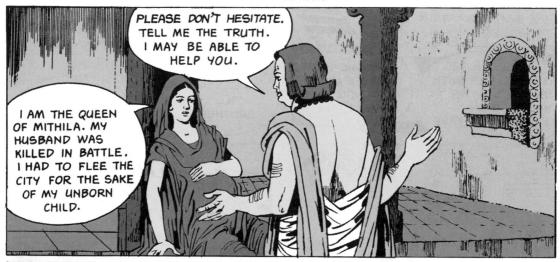

THE BRAHMANA TOOK HER TO HIS WIFE.

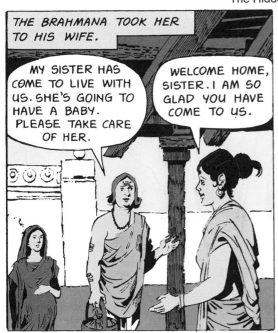

MY SISTER HAS COME TO LIVE WITH US. SHE'S GOING TO HAVE A BABY. PLEASE TAKE CARE OF HER.

WELCOME HOME, SISTER. I AM SO GLAD YOU HAVE COME TO US.

THE BRAHMANA AND HIS WIFE LOOKED AFTER HER WITH LOVE AND CARE. AFTER A FEW DAYS, A SON WAS BORN TO HER.

WHAT SHALL WE CALL HIM, BROTHER?

WE'LL CALL HIM MAHAJANAKA.

THE QUEEN AND HER SON STAYED ON IN THE HOUSE OF THE KIND BRAHMANA AND HIS WIFE.

HOW HAPPY I AM THAT WE ARE STILL ALIVE AND WELL.

WHEN MAHAJANAKA GREW A LITTLE OLDER, HE MADE FRIENDS WITH THE BOYS IN THE NEIGHBOURHOOD.

COME ON, MAHAJANAKA. WE ARE WAITING FOR YOU.

I'M COMING!

BUT THEY OFTEN QUARRELLED TOO. AND, THEN, MAHAJANAKA WHO WAS THE STRONGEST OF THEM ALL, WOULD BEAT UP THE OTHERS. ONE DAY, AFTER SUCH A QUARREL —

I'LL GO AND TELL MY FATHER!

I'LL ALSO GO AND TELL MY...

WHO? WHO WOULD YOU TELL?

YOU HAVE NO FATHER!

HE HAS NO FATHER!

HA! HA!

HE HAS NO FATHER!

MAHAJANAKA RAN TO HIS MOTHER.

MOTHER, THEY SAY I HAVE NO FATHER. THEY SAY...

OH, MOTHER! WHO IS MY FATHER?

I'LL TELL YOU, SON. BUT DON'T CRY. PLEASE DON'T... THAT'S A GOOD BOY!

NOW TELL ME.

HOW CAN I, SON? OUR ENEMIES SHOULDN'T KNOW THAT WE ARE ALIVE! OH, WHAT SHALL I DO?

WHY ARE YOU SILENT, MOTHER? TELL ME! TELL ME THE TRUTH!

YOU ARE THE SON OF KING ARITTHAJANAKA OF MITHILA!

YOU MEAN, I AM A PRINCE!

"YES, YOU ARE A PRINCE. A FEW DAYS BEFORE YOU WERE BORN, YOUR FATHER HAD TO LEAVE TO DO BATTLE WITH HIS ENEMY, POLJANAKA."

IF ANYTHING SHOULD HAPPEN TO ME, YOU MUST PROTECT YOURSELF AND SAVE OUR CHILD.

"I WAITED ANXIOUSLY FOR NEWS OF THE BATTLE. THEN TOWARDS MIDDAY, A MESSENGER RUSHED IN."

WE HAVE LOST ...OUR KING IS NO MORE! POLJANAKA AND HIS MEN WILL BE HERE ANY MOMENT.

THE ENEMY WILL SOON BE HERE!

LET'S SAVE OURSELVES WHILE WE CAN.

MY LADY, I...I...

DO YOU WANT TO LEAVE TOO? I UNDERSTAND. YOU MAY GO.

MY WHOLE WORLD IS CRUMBLING AROUND ME. LIFE HAS NO MEANING ANY MORE. BUT I MUST STAY ALIVE FOR THE SAKE OF OUR CHILD.

"I TIED TOGETHER SOME GOLD COINS AND JEWELS AND PUT THE BUNDLE IN AN OLD BASKET."

8

"AFTER THAT I CAST OFF MY ROYAL CLOTHES, DISGUISED MYSELF AS A MAID AND LEFT THE PALACE WITH THE BASKET."

"A CARTER BROUGHT ME HERE TO KALACHAMPA."

IF IT WERE NOT FOR OUR HOST AND HIS WIFE, I DON'T KNOW WHAT WOULD HAVE HAPPENED TO ME... AND LATER YOU.

EVEN NOW I AM AFRAID OF OUR ENEMIES. NOBODY SHOULD KNOW WHO WE ARE.

DON'T WORRY, MOTHER. NO ONE WILL. I PROMISE.

SOON AFTER THAT, HE STARTED STUDYING UNDER THE BRAHMANA.

I MUST WORK HARD. ONE DAY I WILL RULE OVER MITHILA.

YEARS PASSED. MAHAJANAKA GREW UP TO BE A HANDSOME AND LEARNED MAN. ONE DAY —

MOTHER, DO YOU HAVE ANY MONEY WITH YOU?

I DID NOT COME AWAY FROM MITHILA, EMPTY-HANDED. BUT WHY DO YOU ASK, MY SON?

I WISH TO GO TO MITHILA TO CLAIM MY THRONE.

MY SON, I HAVE BEEN WAITING ALL THESE YEARS FOR THIS DAY!

I HAVE A FEW GOLD COINS AND ORNA-MENTS. THEY ARE ALL YOURS.

NO, MOTHER, NOT ALL. I SHALL TAKE HALF. THE REST YOU MUST KEEP.

WITH MY HALF I SHALL BUY SOME MERCHANDISE, CARRY ON TRADE OVERSEAS AND EARN THE MONEY I'LL NEED, TO RAISE AN ARMY.

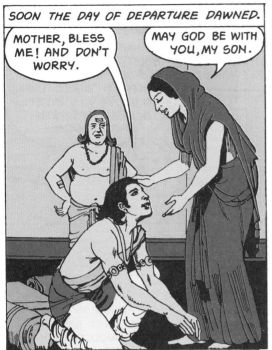

SOON THE DAY OF DEPARTURE DAWNED.

MOTHER, BLESS ME! AND DON'T WORRY.

MAY GOD BE WITH YOU, MY SON.

AS THE SHIP SET SAIL —

I WONDER IF POLJANAKA IS STILL ALIVE. WILL I HAVE TO FIGHT HIM OR HIS SON? I WONDER WHAT AWAITS ME AT MITHILA.

POLJANAKA WAS ALIVE BUT SERIOUSLY ILL AND HE HAD NO SON.

HIS MINISTERS WERE WORRIED ABOUT THE FUTURE OF THE KINGDOM.

WHY DON'T WE ASK THE KING TO APPOINT A SUCCESSOR?

SO THEY WENT TO THE KING.

I HAVE GIVEN THE MATTER DEEP THOUGHT AND MADE MY DECISION. THE MAN MY DAUGHTER CHOOSES FOR A HUSBAND, SHALL BE THE KING.

YOUR MAJESTY, PRINCESS SHIVALI WILL CHOOSE A GOOD MAN BUT HOW CAN WE BE SURE THAT HE WILL MAKE A GOOD KING?

I HAVE THOUGHT ABOUT THAT TOO. HER SUITOR WILL HAVE TO PERFORM THREE TASKS TO PROVE HIS INTELLIGENCE, STRENGTH AND WISDOM.

FIRST, HE MUST POINT OUT THE HEAD OF THE PRINCESS' SQUARE BED. THEN HE MUST STRING A BOW WHICH WOULD ORDINARILY REQUIRE THE STRENGTH OF A THOUSAND MEN.

LASTLY, WITH THE HELP OF SIXTEEN CLUES, HE WILL HAVE TO FIND THE SIXTEEN POTS OF GOLD I'VE HIDDEN IN AND AROUND THE PALACE.

YOU MUST LET THE PRINCESS MARRY HIM, ONLY IF HE SUCCEEDS IN PERFORMING ALL THE TASKS.

A FEW DAYS LATER THE KING DIED.

HOW DO WE GO ABOUT FINDING A HUSBAND FOR SHIVALI? SHOULD WE SEND OUT MESSENGERS?

FIRST LET US SEE IF OUR HANDSOME YOUNG GENERAL PLEASES HER.

SOME TIME LATER—

O PRINCESS, YOUR FATHER LIKED THE GENERAL VERY MUCH. THE MINISTERS WANT YOU TO...

ASK THE GENERAL TO SEE ME AT ONCE.

THE GENERAL WAS DELIGHTED TO RECEIVE THE PRINCESS ORDER.

SHE WANTS TO SEE ME! I'M THE MAN SHIVALI HAS CHOSEN TO MARRY! THE FUTURE KING OF MITHILA!

IN HIS ANXIETY NOT TO KEEP THE PRINCESS WAITING HE RAN UP THE STAIRS.

HE LACKS COMPOSURE AND DIGNITY.

SOON THE GENERAL STOOD BEFORE HER.

I AM AT YOUR SERVICE, PRINCESS.

WHAT CAN YOU DO FOR ME?

OH! ANYTHING! YOUR WORD IS MY COMMAND!

AH! IS THAT SO?

YES... I'LL STRIVE TO SERVE YOU IN EVERY WAY—EVEN PRESS YOUR FEET OR FETCH YOUR SLIPPERS!

I COULD NEVER RESPECT THIS SERVILE CREATURE!

HOW CAN YOU BE SO MEEK! HAVE YOU NO SELF-RESPECT? YOU MAY GO NOW, GENERAL!

WHEN THE GENERAL RETURNED TO THE MINISTERS —

WHAT HAPPENED? YOU LOOK CREST-FALLEN!

THAT GIRL IS HARD TO PLEASE!

PERHAPS THE TREASURER MIGHT SUCCEED WHERE THE GENERAL FAILED.

YES. HE IS WISE... AND HANDSOME.

SO THE TREASURER WAS SENT TO MEET THE PRINCESS. BUT HE TOO FAILED. SO DID ALL·THE OTHERS WHO TRIED TO WOO HER.

MEANWHILE ON BOARD MAHAJANAKA'S SHIP—

THE SEA HAS SUDDENLY BECOME ROUGH. IT LOOKS AS IF IT'S GOING TO RAIN!

SOON, A STORM BROKE. WAVE AFTER MIGHTY WAVE LASHED AT THE SHIP.

I MUST REMAIN CALM! I MUST NOT PANIC.

HE MOVED NEARER THE MAST AND HELD ON TO IT WITH ALL HIS STRENGTH.

I HAVE A MISSION TO ACCOMPLISH. I MUST NOT LET DEATH ROB ME OF THE CHANCE TO REGAIN THE THRONE OF MITHILA.

AS THE SHIP SANK UNDER THE ONSLAUGHT OF THE WAVES, MAHAJANAKA TIGHTENED HIS GRIP ON THE MAST.

I WON'T GIVE UP! I WILL SURVIVE THIS ORDEAL. I MUST.

A FEW DAYS LATER, MAHA-JANAKA WAS WASHED ASHORE. WHEN HE OPENED HIS EYES —

WHERE AM I? WHAT AN EFFORT IT IS TO MOVE! BUT I MUST MUSTER ALL MY STRENGTH AND FIND MY WAY TO THE CITY.

LATER, IN A GARDEN OUTSIDE THE EASTERN GATE OF THE CITY, HE OVERHEARD TWO MEN TALKING.

...AND SO MITHILA IS STILL WITHOUT A KING!

WHAT'S THIS I HEAR!

I AM IN MITHILA! AND MITHILA IS WITHOUT A KING!

BUT I HAVE NEITHER WEAPONS NOR MONEY. I MUST MOVE CAUTIOUSLY. I MUST LIE DOWN AND GET SOME REST BEFORE I MAKE ANY PLANS.

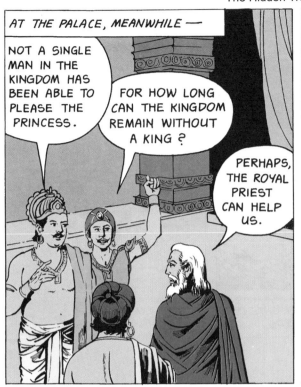

AT THE PALACE, MEANWHILE —

NOT A SINGLE MAN IN THE KINGDOM HAS BEEN ABLE TO PLEASE THE PRINCESS.

FOR HOW LONG CAN THE KINGDOM REMAIN WITHOUT A KING?

PERHAPS, THE ROYAL PRIEST CAN HELP US.

WHEN THEY CONSULTED THE ROYAL PRIEST —

SEND OUT THE SACRED CHARIOT. IT WILL LEAD US TO THE RIGHT MAN.

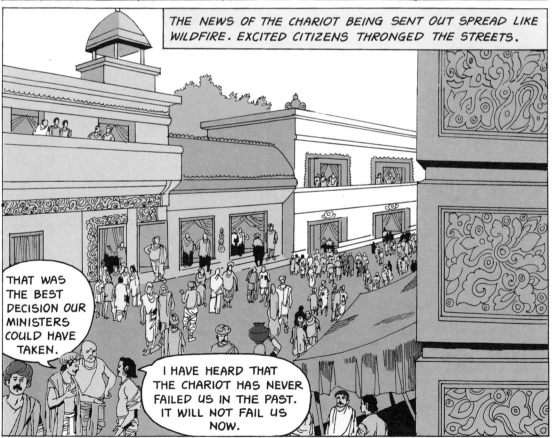

THE NEWS OF THE CHARIOT BEING SENT OUT SPREAD LIKE WILDFIRE. EXCITED CITIZENS THRONGED THE STREETS.

THAT WAS THE BEST DECISION OUR MINISTERS COULD HAVE TAKEN.

I HAVE HEARD THAT THE CHARIOT HAS NEVER FAILED US IN THE PAST. IT WILL NOT FAIL US NOW.

AT THE AUSPICIOUS HOUR THE ROYAL PRIEST STOOD BEFORE THE CHARIOT.

LEAD US TO HIM WHO WILL PLEASE SHIVALI AND WHO IS FIT TO RULE A KINGDOM.

THE ROYAL PRIEST WITH THE MINISTERS WALKED BEHIND THE CHARIOT AS IT ROLLED PAST THE HOUSES OF THE GENERAL, THE TREASURER, AND ALL THE OTHER SUITORS.

SUDDENLY THE HORSES BROKE INTO A GALLOP.

DON'T TRY TO SLOW THEM DOWN. WE'LL KEEP PACE WITH THEM.

THE CHARIOT SPED ON TOWARDS THE EASTERN GATE OF THE CITY...

...AND THEN ENTERING THE GARDEN...

...CAME TO A HALT NEAR THE SPOT WHERE MAHAJANAKA LAY SLEEPING.

THE CHARIOT HAS NEVER FAILED US...BUT...HE'S A TOTAL STRANGER.

I HAVE AN IDEA. LET THE DRUMS BE BEATEN AND THE HORNS BE BLOWN. LET THERE BE A DEAFENING UPROAR.

HOW HE WAKES UP, WHAT HE DOES AND SAYS, WILL TELL US MUCH ABOUT HIM. HE'S STIRRING!

THE NOISE AROUND HIM AWOKE MAHAJANAKA.

WHAT A TERRIBLE DIN! WHY ARE ALL THESE PEOPLE HERE? HM..M.M. I'LL KNOW SOONER OR LATER.

WHEN THE DIN AWOKE HIM THERE WAS NO SIGN OF PANIC IN HIS EYES. THEN HE WENT BACK TO SLEEP WITHOUT BETRAYING THE SLIGHTEST CURIOSITY. HE EXPECTS AN EXPLANATION FROM US AND IS CONFIDENT OF GETTING IT. HE IS BRAVE, WISE AND NOBLE.

THE PRIEST CAME FORWARD.

RISE, O NOBLE ONE. THE KINGDOM AWAITS YOU!

WHEN MAHAJANAKA SAT UP, THE PRIEST EXPLAINED ALL TO HIM.

ARE YOU WILLING TO WOO OUR PRINCESS AND ATTEMPT THE TASKS?

I AM. LET'S GO TO THE PALACE.

LED BY MAHAJANAKA WHO WAS SEATED IN THE CHARIOT, THE PROCESSION WENDED ITS WAY TO THE PALACE.

LONG LIVE THE KING!

WHEN PRINCESS SHIVALI WAS TOLD ABOUT MAHAJANAKA —

A TOTAL STRANGER? THE CHARIOT MAY HAVE FOUND HIM TO BE THE RIGHT MAN. BUT WILL I? ASK HIM TO SEE ME AT ONCE.

SHIVALI'S MAID DID AS SHE WAS TOLD.

THE PRINCESS WANTS TO SEE YOU.

BUT MAHAJANAKA DID NOT MOVE. SOON ANOTHER MAID CAME IN.

THE PRINCESS IS WAITING FOR YOU IN HER CHAMBER.

ONLY WHEN A THIRD MAID BROUGHT THE SAME MESSAGE DID HE RESPOND.

TELL HER I'LL COME IN A MOMENT. ONE OF YOU STAY WITH ME AND SHOW ME THE WAY.

HE TOOK HIS OWN TIME TO GET UP AND WALKED SLOWLY, REGALLY TOWARDS THE PRINCESS' ROOM.

HE DELIBERATELY KEPT THE PRINCESS WAITING.

PERHAPS, THAT'S WHAT THE PRINCESS EXPECTED OF A SUITOR!

AS MAHAJANAKA WALKED AT A LEISURELY PACE UP THE STAIRS LEADING TO SHIVALI'S ROOM —

SHE IS TRYING TO GUAGE ME. WELL...LET HER! I AM SURE SHE WON'T BE DISAPPOINTED.

HOW SERENE AND CONFIDENT HIS MANNER! HOW MAJESTIC! HE IS THE MAN FOR ME!

SHE CAME OUT TO GREET HIM.

WELCOME, MY LORD!

LITTLE DID I DREAM THAT TO REGAIN MITHILA, I WOULD HAVE TO WIN THE RESPECT OF A PRINCESS AND NOT A BATTLE!

WON'T YOU COME IN? I'LL SEND FOR THE MINISTERS.

WHEN THE MINISTERS CAME —

HOW PLEASED WE ARE TO KNOW THAT OUR PRINCESS HAS WELCOMED YOU.

THE CHARIOT WAS RIGHT AS USUAL.

NOW FOR THE TASKS. FIRST YOU WILL HAVE TO FIND THE HEAD OF A SQUARE BED.

IS THAT ALL?

WHERE IS THE BED? PLEASE SHOW IT TO ME.

IT'S IN THERE.

WHEN THEY WENT INSIDE —

MAY I RELAX HERE FOR A WHILE?

OF COURSE, MY LORD!

HE SAT DOWN ON THE BED AND HELD OUT A PIN.

WHERE...? WHERE SHALL I KEEP THIS, SHIVALI?

GIVE IT TO ME.

I MUST SUCCEED IN PERFORMING ALL THE TASKS AS MUCH FOR MAKING THIS INTELLIGENT, GRACIOUS GIRL MY WIFE AS FOR MAKING THE THRONE OF MITHILA MINE.

SOMETHING TELLS ME THAT HE'S GOING TO SUCCEED. AND I HOPE WITH ALL MY HEART THAT HE DOES.

THAT—THE PLACE WHERE SHIVALI WOULD NATURALLY PRESERVE HER PINS WHEN SHE REMOVES THEM—IS THE HEAD OF THE BED.

IT IS. HE IS RIGHT.

I HOPE THE NEXT TASK IS A MORE CHALLENGING ONE.

YOU'LL HAVE TO STRING THE GREAT BOW.

THEY WENT TO THE ARMOURY. THERE MAHAJANAKA WAS SHOWN THE BOW. HE LIFTED IT UP WITH EASE.

24

HE'S STRUNG IT! IT'S INCREDIBLE!

WELL DONE, MY LORD!

AND NOW?

THE LAST TEST. YOU HAVE TO FIND THE SIXTEEN POTS OF GOLD HIDDEN IN AND AROUND THE PALACE.

ARE THERE ANY CLUES?

YES, THERE ARE. YOU WILL FIND THE FIRST POT...

...WHERE THE SUN RISES; AND THE SECOND WHERE THE SUN SETS. THE THIRD...

THE MINISTER GAVE HIM THE REST OF THE CLUES. THEN —

FOR THIS TASK, I'LL NEED SOME TIME. BUT I'M SURE I'LL FIND ALL SIXTEEN POTS.

WE SINCERELY HOPE YOU DO.

THAT NIGHT MAHAJANAKA THOUGHT VERY HARD.

WHERE THE SUN RISES ...AND WHERE IT SETS..HMM ...THESE CAN'T SIMPLY BE EAST AND WEST. WHAT COULD IT BE...? SUN...

...SUN...SUN... THAT'S IT! THE SUN ALSO SYMBOLIZES LIGHT — THE LIGHT OF KNOWLEDGE AND TRUTH. NOW I KNOW!

THE NEXT MORNING WHEN THE MINISTERS ASSEMBLED IN THE HALL —

I'LL TRY TO FIND THE POTS TODAY. BUT, FIRST, I'D LIKE TO KNOW JUST ONE THING.

DID YOUR KING HONOUR ASCETICS AND SCHOLARS?

OH YES, HE DID! HE ALWAYS WORSHIPPED THEM LIKE GODS.

WHERE DID HE RECEIVE THEM WHEN THEY CAME?

COME WITH US, AND WE'LL SHOW YOU THE PLACE.

THE MINISTERS TOOK HIM OUTSIDE THE PALACE.

THIS IS WHERE THE KING RECEIVED ASCETICS AND SCHOLARS.

HAVE THIS PLACE DUG UP AND YOU WILL FIND THE FIRST POT.

THE PLACE WAS DUG UP. SOON —

LOOK! A HUGE POT!

REALLY? PULL IT UP QUICKLY.

THE POT WAS LIFTED UP AND OPENED.

GOLD! AND THERE ARE FIFTEEN MORE LIKE THIS.

NOW WHERE DID HE SEE THEM OFF?

THEY TOOK HIM TO THE SPOT.

THE KING ALWAYS ACCOMPANIED THEM UP TO THIS POINT. THIS IS WHERE HE SAW THEM OFF.

HMM! HAVE THIS PLACE DUG UP AND YOU'LL FIND THE SECOND POT.

27

AND TRUE ENOUGH THEY DID.

HOW DID YOU KNOW THAT THESE WERE THE SPOTS, MY LORD?

THE SUN MENTIONED BY THE KING IS NOT THE SUN WE KNOW. HE MEANT THE SUN OF KNOWLEDGE WITH WHICH SCHOLARS SHINE.

AFTER THIS MAHAJANAKA DECIPHERED THE REMAINING CLUES ONE AFTER THE OTHER AND ALL THE SIXTEEN POTS WERE FOUND.

YOU HAVE PROVED YOURSELF ON EVERY SCORE, MY LORD. YOU MUST NOW MARRY THE PRINCESS, AND MAKE US HAPPY.

THAT WILL HAVE TO WAIT FOR A WHILE.

FIRST, I WANT MY MOTHER AND MY UNCLE TO BE BROUGHT HERE FROM KALACHAMPA. PLEASE SEND SOMEONE TO FETCH THEM.

IT SHALL BE DONE AT ONCE.

AFTER A FEW WEEKS THE BRAHMANA ARRIVED WITH MAHAJANAKA'S MOTHER.

I AM SO HAPPY, SON. YOU HAVE DONE IT!

MOTHER!

MAHAJANAKA TURNED TO SHIVALI —

SHIVALI, MOTHER HAS COME HOME TODAY. SHE WAS THE QUEEN OF MITHILA ONCE.

WELCOME, MOTHER.

HE IS THE SON OF A KING! NO WONDER!

LATER, MAHAJANAKA AND SHIVALI WERE MARRIED.

WHAT A WELL-MATCHED COUPLE! HAD I NOT RUN AWAY FROM HERE WHEN MY LORD DIED, I WOULDN'T HAVE SEEN THIS DAY.

WHEN MAHAJANAKA WAS CROWNED KING OF MITHILA, HE MADE AN ANNOUNCEMENT—

I DECLARE THAT THE GOLD FOUND IN THE POTS WILL BE DISTRIBUTED AMONG THE NEEDY.

THE DECLARATION WAS RECEIVED WITH GREAT JOY.

LONG LIVE KING MAHAJANAKA!!

OUR KING IS SO GENEROUS!

YES, AND WISE AND VALIANT TOO!

LATER —

MOTHER, BY GIVING AWAY THE GOLD TO THE NEEDY, I HAVE FOUND A MORE VALUABLE TREASURE —THE GOODWILL AND BLESSINGS OF MY PEOPLE!

YOU ARE RIGHT, MY SON.

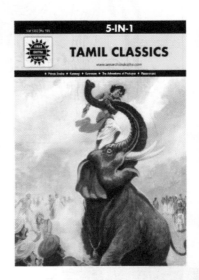

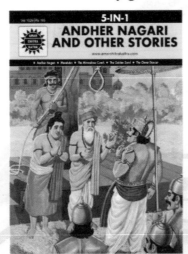

SUBSCRIBE NOW!

TINKLE COMBO
MAGAZINE + DIGEST
1 year subscription

Pay only
~~₹1200~~
₹880!

FREE
2 Time Compass DVDs worth ₹598

TINKLE
MAGAZINE
1 year subscription

Pay only
~~₹480~~
₹380!

I would like a one year subscription for
TINKLE COMBO ☐ **TINKLE MAGAZINE** ☐
(Please tick the appropriate box)

YOUR DETAILS*

Name: .... Date of Birth: |__| / |__| / |_____|

Address: ....

.... City: .... Pin: |__|__|__|__|__|__| State: ....

School: .... Class: ....

Tel: .... Mobile: + 91 - |__|__|__|__|__|__|__|__|__|__|

Email: .... Signature: ....

PAYMENT OPTIONS

☐ Cheque /DD:

Please find enclosed Cheque /DD no. |__|__|__|__|__|__| drawn in favour of 'ACK Media Direct Pvt. Ltd.'

at .... (bank) for the amount .... ,

dated |__|__| / |__|__| / |__|__|__|__| and send it to: IBH Books & Magazines Distributers Pvt. Ltd., Arch No. 30,
West Approach, Below Mahalaxmi Bridge, Mahalaxmi (W), Mumbai - 400034.

☐ Pay Cash on Delivery: Pay cash on delivery of the first issue to the postman. (Additional charge of ₹50 applicable)

☐ Pay by money order: Pay by money order in favour of "ACK Media Direct Pvt. Ltd."

☐ Online subscription: Please visit: www.amarchitrakatha.com

For any queries or further information: Email: customerservice@ack-media.com or Call: 022-40497435 / 36